NEW TAB

RH

New Tab

GUILLAUME MORISSETTE

ESPLANADE
Books
THE FICTION SERIES AT VÉHICULE PRESS

Published with the generous assistance of the Canada Council for the Arts, the Canada Book Fund of the Department of Canadian Heritage, and the Société de développement des entreprises culturelles du Québec (SODEC).

Cover design: David Drummond
Photo of author: Sarah O'Driscoll
Typeset in Minion by Simon Garamond
Printed by Marquis Printing Inc.

LIBRARY AND ARCHIVES CANADA CATALOGUING IN PUBLICATION

Morissette, Guillaume, author
New tab / Guillaume Morissette.

ISBN 978-1-55065-372-4 (PBK.)
ISBN: 978-1-55065-393-9 (EPUB.)

I. Title.

PS8626.O7498N49 2014   C813'.6   C2014-900592-X

Published by Véhicule Press, Montréal, Québec, Canada
www.vehiculepress.com

Distribution in Canada by LitDistCo
www.litdistco.ca

Distributed in the U.S. by Independent Publishers Group
www.ipgbook.com

Printed in Canada on FSC certified paper

ACKNOWLEDGEMENTS

Thank you Ashley Opheim, Laura Broadbent, Lucy K. Shaw, Simona Lepadatu, Stacey Teague, Hannah Van Arsdale, Madeleine Black, Jill Walsh, Sarah O'Driscoll, Tyler Crawford, Frankie Barnet, Aeron MacHattie, Arielle Gavin, Chelle Whitchurch, Michael J. Seidlinger, Simon Dardick & Andrew Steinmetz.

STALKING BRENT ON FACEBOOK, I saw from his profile picture that he was tall and had sloppy bed hair that randomly looked excellent and that he owned a MacBook and a t-shirt that said "RIP DJ Screw." I looked for a birth year but there was no year specified, just a month and a day. I didn't know if he was younger than me or maybe my age. I wanted him to be my age. I wanted him to be ten thousand years older than me. I wanted him to be ten thousand years older than me and still a mess and still thinking things like, "I am the shittiest person alive," on a regular basis.

That year, I kept meeting people who I thought were my age but then turned out to be younger than me. Brent was a good example. He was a fully-grown human person, looked like more of a dad than I ever would, but then somewhere in my thought process I felt the defeating certitude that Brent was, in fact, a year or two younger than me.

It was confusing information to handle.

"Mid-twenties and not insane and drama-free," is how I had described myself to Brent over email. His email address ended with the domain name of a local arts and culture festival. His Craigslist ad had said that he was an independent filmmaker who was sharing a house with an art student and an "awesome guy trying to figure out life." They had a room available and I had a person available. Just from the emails with Brent, I already felt good about it and like I wanted to take it.

Later that day, I received two emails from him in the span of maybe an hour. The first email was to ask me when I could come by to visit and the second email was to tell me they had filled the room and that it wouldn't work out. Brent explained that they needed someone right away and that a person had offered to pay cash if he could take the room immediately. Staring at Brent's second email, I felt doomed. I never had good timing, wouldn't luck into a new living situation I would like, would just end up settling for one that I thought was okay but then would eventually grow to loathe, with no one there to teach me how to have sloppy bed hair that randomly looks excellent.

Then I thought, "It's December, everyone feels doomed in December."

This is how it felt: I still had some leftover youth, but by that point I had lived enough years, enough decades to feel like I wanted reality to go away for a while, make me miss it a little.

Reality was a kind of insomnia, always there, just there, annoyingly there, in my bed, at the park, inside every raccoon, behind movie stars in movie trailers, there, being, occurring, fluctuating, not telling me what it wanted from me, giving me the silent treatment, a kind of torture. "What?" I wanted to scream at it. Closing my eyes didn't make it go away, because what I saw then wasn't the absence of reality, it was only closed eyelids.

There was nothing I could do to hurt reality. I couldn't set it on fire, couldn't put it up for auction on eBay, couldn't pump it full of helium and then wave it goodbye while driving away in a lime-green Jeep Wrangler. I couldn't separate myself from reality. I would always be trapped within.

It was a terrible sensation, though only when I thought about it.

"We're just off of St-Dominique and Mont-Royal," read Ines' third email, "but we also have a bit of an evil situation right now. I'll explain in person. I hope that's okay."

"That's okay," I typed. I was sitting on my bed with my back resting against a pillow. It was the third week of January. The laptop was testing my thighs' resistance to heat. The pillow was rectangular and the computer screen was also rectangular.

"I could come by on Sunday if you want," I typed. "Maybe two p.m."

About half an hour later, I received a response email from Ines to confirm the time and date. I closed two browser tabs, looked at the cropped heads of people on Facebook for a while, didn't feel optimistic about going to see another room, didn't feel anything. Two days before, I had visited an overly communal eleven and a half. One of the roommates there had seemed excited that I owned an Xbox 360, because he also owned an Xbox 360.

"I got so smashed last night," read a Chat message from Shannon on Facebook. "Oh my god. I need an IV bag. Plug it in my brain, through my nose."

"I kind of wish I was regretting last night right now," I typed back. "I didn't get your text until this morning. My phone fucked me over. I would have come."

"I am never going out again," typed Shannon. "I kind of want to go out tonight. But maybe I need to stay in and watch that movie I bought when the Blockbuster closed down. I still haven't watched it."

"I might just hide in my room tonight," I typed. "I can't decide if that's Zen or depressing."

"Is it really four?" typed Shannon. "I don't know if I trust what time now is."

"I know what you mean," I typed. "Winter is terrible. Every day feels vaguely like a Wednesday, and any time of the day feels vaguely like four p.m."

"The Concordia website makes no sense," typed Shannon. "No sense at all. I need the form for the external credit thing but I've looked everywhere and it's not everywhere I've looked."

"Most of the time, I just google 'Concordia' and then the thing I am looking for," I typed. "Google finds it. Concordia's search engine is programmed to hate people. But it's not its fault. It's the programming's fault."

"One of these days I am going to ram my car into Concordia," typed Shannon. "Not voluntarily or involuntarily, more like, I'll just let it happen."

"I would defend you in court," I typed. "It was provocation, I would say."

"You could say I was messed up at an early age," typed Shannon, "by my kindergarten teacher. She asked us to draw something starting with the letter W, so I drew Wakko from the *Animaniacs*. My teacher said I had made that up. She made me draw a whale. A stupid whale."

"That's funny," I typed. "On Thursday, someone in my creative process class asked the teacher what you can do with a creative writing degree. He said, 'Nothing,' and then laughed. Other people laughed nervously."

"That's true," typed Shannon. "I mean, our lives are poorly planned. Realistically, I don't know how I'll be hired for anything after I graduate. If you're a girl, it's even worse. All the women poets seem to end up locked in asylums or offing themselves."

"We should give up while we still can," I typed. "Move to Sweden, change both our first names to Knut."

"It's tempting," typed Shannon.

"In November, I met this guy who works at Blizzarts," I typed. "He had just graduated as an English lit. major. His boss didn't expect him to write essays that questioned things. His boss wanted him to cut lemons."

"Ugh," typed Shannon. "I don't understand why people aren't more concerned about this. They spend all their time instead being catty and backtalking other people's writing."

"Do you think people in other programs are less insecure?" I typed.

"People in Fine Arts are probably like, 'Did you see the abstract shapes that this bitch submitted to class? I hate that bitch,'" typed Shannon. "No, you're right. It's probably the same thing."

As a human being, I wasn't good at anything obvious, didn't foresee a direct path like, "I can paint, so I am going to be a painter." I could think interesting things from time to time, but then how should the thoughts be used? I could be inventive just as much as I could be a disaster. My skill set was still a complete mystery to me, felt like a rarely observed phenomenon, something that could be just a fluke or an elaborate hoax.

Meeting fully grown human beings with ridiculous, implausible birth years was starting to impose itself as the default mode of meeting new people.

On certain days, it seemed like one hundred percent of what I looked at on the internet was, when I thought about it, deeply embarrassing.

I made tea in the kitchen by pouring hot water on a white bag in the shape of a trapezoid. It was ten a.m. Coming through the window was a kind of trembling light, as if nervous a little, afraid to get yelled at or scolded. I couldn't get myself to feel awake. I would never feel awake. I thought about dynamiting my leg to feel awake. I didn't have dynamite.

I heard two of my roommates moving around in their rooms. Our apartment was maybe eighty percent hallways, with rooms spread out far apart from one another, making it easier for us to avoid each other than to hang out. This was okay, as I was more comfortable with their absence than with their presence. They were all, like me, French Canadian. Two of them had jobs and complained about them and sometimes had people over, to complain about other jobs than theirs. One, unlike me, had separatist ideals and a romantic attachment to French Canadian culture. I think she resented me a little for not voting and not being proud by default of my cultural heritage and for having applied to an English-speaking university instead of a French-speaking one. What we both didn't understand at the time was that switching to English as a primary language was just a practical way for me to reinvent myself.

I had lived there for about a year in my first apartment in Montreal, felt ready to move out, wanted those people, my roommates, to no longer be people in my life, just memories, abstractions in my head locked behind some sort of mental door labelled, "Caution, harmful radiation, do not open."

In the metro maybe two hours later, I read about twenty pages of *The Hour of the Star* by Clarice Lispector. In the novella, an unhappy person seemed unable to perceive herself as unhappy. I got out at the Mont-Royal station and walked with my head down, watching my feet compress snow. Around me, wind felt overexcited, eager to be elsewhere, moving things around as if trying to solve some sort of imperceptible puzzle. I blew heat onto my fingers and then couldn't think of a good reason that justified not wearing mittens.

I turned on St-Dominique and passed a garage door with purple graffiti on it that said "Ghostbusters." I found a white door located at ground level with the address I was looking for above it. Scotch-taped to the door's window was a cut-out article from a local newspaper about what looked like a local independent short film I had never heard of. I knocked and then thought about rearranging my hair and then regretted knocking right away and then someone opened the door. A person wearing a beige blouse with butterflies on it greeted me and introduced herself as Ines. "Thomas," I said. My own name echoed in my head. I tried smiling but couldn't produce something high enough for it to be a smile, just a kind of weird mouth extension, something I could take back, pretend had never happened, my little secret.

I entered, removed my jacket and winter things. Ines guided me around. She listed the pros and cons of each room and explained the rent system and the electric bill system. There was a large bedroom, an average-sized bedroom with a walk-in closet, a small bedroom with natural light but no closet, a small bedroom with no natural light but a closet, a common area, a kitchen, a bathroom. The residence didn't feel like an apartment so much as a house, except maybe narrower, as if it had been, somehow, deflated, to occupy less space, like an air mattress.

"Our internet is free," said Ines. "There's a Wi-Fi signal somewhere around that's not protected. At first, Cristian was like, 'Don't use it, it's a trap.' He thought it was too good to be true. But then we started using it anyway and nothing happened, so we just kept going."

Behind the building was a medium-sized backyard that contained a depressing amount of snow, a metal staircase that spiralled like a pig's tail, a shed, what looked like stacks of chairs unlikely to survive winter, and a plastic flamingo, though its body was submerged and only the head was visible. I wasn't expecting a backyard at all, so I was kind of impressed by it.

In the area, most buildings didn't have backyards, just touched each other uncomfortably instead.

"In the summer, we sometimes use the space for movie screenings," Ines said. "It's great."

Looking into the backyard again, I noticed a homemade movie screen made from two by fours and a large piece of cloth. I glanced back at Ines. She smiled. I thought about how she had been smiling a lot, easily and naturally, as if for her that didn't require any effort at all. I felt jealous a little. We walked back to the common area. Around us were a cat clock, a square pillow with kittens on it, Christmas lights, a stained couch, a small television monitor, a thermostat with a cat sticker on it and about thirty miniature stuffed jellyfish hanging via strings from the ceiling. Ines explained the jellyfish were originally a project for school. I remembered her mentioning over email that she was a studio arts major.

We sat down. I thought about the jellyfish. I wasn't sure what a group of jellyfish was called. I thought, "a crew," but then didn't think that was correct. "A crew of jellyfish." I noticed my stress level was low, which was good, and that I didn't seem to be feeling uncomfortable or self-conscious. In the past, the process of being interviewed for a room had made me feel like I was being observed and judged and critiqued and, overall, as if a dog in a dog show.

"So another thing I need to explain is why we have a room available now," said Ines.

She paused and placed her hands on her lap.

"I don't even know where to start," she added. "We have to kick Dan out. He's the evil situation I was talking about. He moved in a few weeks ago but he's being really creepy. We're scared of him now. He's forty. Dan's forty."

Ines explained that Dan worked two days per week doing something no one understood. On most days, he sat on the couch, ate salted crackers, monitored the small television monitor, complained a lot. He was impossible to avoid.

"He's like a black hole," said Ines. "The sexist shit he told me, it's unbelievable. He also got into a screaming argument with Cristian about something. Cristian is never stressed or angry about anything, so I don't even know how he did that. We just don't want to have to deal with him anymore."

Trying to visualize Dan, I thought, "Black hole." I pictured a large celestial object hovering five inches above the stained couch, devouring time, matter and space, watching judgmental daytime television, seeking life advice from the commercials.

"How did you find him?" I said.

"Our other roommate is in South America for two months," said Ines. "He's the one who interviewed him. Dan was willing to pay cash right away so he said yes. When Dan moved in, we immediately thought that there was something wrong with him. He had a bag of dirty clothes and that was it. He was like, 'Do you guys have a mattress for me?' We had one but it was like, how can you be forty and not own anything?"

Ines paused again. She added that she thought Dan had maybe just got out of prison.

"But he'll be gone before the end of the month, so you don't have to worry about that," said Ines. "Right now, living here, there's me, Cristian and Niklas, who's subletting. Niklas is twenty and from Germany. He's adorable. It's his first time living by himself. He wanted to get life experience before starting university in Germany, so all he does is go out and party a lot. There's also Brent, who Niklas is replacing for now. Brent is amazing. He's the one in South America."

"Wait, is he a filmmaker?" I said.

"Yes, do you know him?" said Ines. "His last name is Cole."

"I think we emailed," I said. "That's funny. I replied to his ad a few weeks ago. He wanted me to visit. Then he emailed me again saying the room was filled. That was probably Dan."

"And you found your way back," said Ines. "Like a lost cat. That's amazing. Meant to be."

"It's like a bad John Cusack movie," I said.

Ines laughed a little. I thought, "Bad John Cusack movie," and then, "John Cusack movie," and wasn't sure I could tell the difference. I didn't know if Ines was laughing politely or had understood that I was referring to the movie *Serendipity*. In the film, a series of highly improbable coincidences allows John Cusack to reunite with a person he wants to have sex with. "It's romantic," a girl I had watched the movie with had told me in defence of it. After that movie or some other movie, I had stopped watching movies altogether. I wondered if the true purpose of me watching *Serendipity* with John Cusack was to make an awkward offhand reference to it many years later in an earnest attempt to convince Ines that I was not a deranged person and that we should live together.

"What about you, what's your situation?" said Ines. "You said you were at Concordia."

"I am," I said. "I just started school again. I am only part-time for now, though. I am not on loans or anything, so I also have a full-time job."

"What do you study?" said Ines.

"Creative writing," I said.

"That's cool," said Ines. "Your English is good, you just have a little accent. Because of your last name, I wasn't sure if you were going to speak French or not. We mostly communicate in English. Cristian can speak some French, but he only really uses it at work. I am from

Edmonton originally, so I only know a few things. *Permettez-moi, monsieur. Le petit gâteau. La mer Morte.*"

"I am bilingual, so it should be fine," I said.

"That's what I figured," said Ines. "You go to Concordia and stuff." She paused again. I rearranged my hair with my hand. Looking directly at Ines, I noticed a shine in the upper section of her right eye. It looked photoshopped in, as if the shine was on a layer above the eyeball.

"So," said Ines. "Do you have more questions?"

"No," I said. "I think I am good. Do you have more questions for me?"

"Yeah," said Ines. "Do you want the room?"

"I think so, yeah," I said.

"That's great," said Ines. "I really don't want to interview a million people and you seem fine. My email inbox right now is filled with weirdos telling me their life stories and then asking me for directions on how to come here. We haven't told Dan that he's getting kicked out yet, but this week, Cristian and me are going to sit down and drink beers and talk ourselves into it. We've been avoiding it, like I am scared he's going to flip his shit. He might get violent and break stuff."

"Maybe he'll break something from his room," I said.

"He doesn't have anything," said Ines.

"He could flip the mattress over," I said. "Stab it with his keys or something."

"I don't know what he's going to do," said Ines. "When I was a kid and I had to do something I was scared of doing, my mom used to hand me a piece of paper and a pen and tell me, 'Draw courage,' and then I would draw what it would be like to be courageous in that situation. I feel like I should do that now."

"I hope it works out," I said.

"Don't worry," said Ines. "The next week and a half is going to suck, but hopefully he doesn't do anything stupid and then this all just goes away, like a bad dream."

The more I gave to the internet, the better.

I didn't know what I wanted, all I knew was how poorly I felt without it.

Romantically, I still felt like a five-year-old, one that confused fantasy with reality, was afraid of darkness, loud noises. I had spent my high school years being awkward and not handsome and thinking that love and sex and relationships would happen to me eventually, that all I had to do was to avoid thinking about it too much and just wait. Since then, I had had girlfriends and ambiguous relationships and other things, but those had weirdly bounced off of me like a kind of minor deflection. It seemed like I was still waiting and would continue waiting, quietly waiting, like I was in love with the waiting and would miss the waiting if I were to get into a relationship I felt anything other than indifference towards.

I had learned English, my second language, almost by accident, from television sitcoms and role-playing video games. For some reason, I seemed to enjoy speaking English more than I did French, even though in conversation my French accent came out from time to time, or I would search for a word or expression and couldn't think of it and had to stall mid-sentence while trying to remember, which was anxiety-causing and felt like looking for a light switch in the dark, groping the walls at random, hoping to stumble onto the switch.

A meteor shaped like my head, colliding with my head.

On a billboard at work, someone had put up a small poster with company values on it. "Endurance," read one of them. It felt like what they meant was, "How long can you endure being deprived of meaningful work?"

For a while, I had wanted video games to be a career for me, but then games changed or I changed or something changed, and I began to feel like what I was doing with my life was odd, unfulfilling. Moving to Montreal and starting a new job at a studio that mass-produced video games and employed about six hundred people had only accentuated this sensation. The office I worked in was overwhelmingly clean-looking, overly air-conditioned, many shades of grey, filled with desks that were shiny and curvilinear and looked like something out of an alien vessel. I didn't know most of the employees occupying the desks around mine, wasn't even sure what their jobs were. Like me, they didn't talk much, clicked on things at a normal speed, looked focused but not stressed.

It was a lonely work environment.

On my work computer, I checked my email account and then Facebook account and then Twitter account. I thought about how those three actions had become synonymous with opening a computer. "We told Dan that he needed to be out by the end of the month," read an email from Ines. "He didn't want to at first. He yelled, 'This kind of bullshit wouldn't fly in Ontario.' He said that less than two weeks of notice was illegal because he had been living with us for more than ten days, which I don't think is a thing. At some point, he got tired of arguing and just gave up and said he would move out. Living with sketchy roommate is really awkward now. Thus comical. It's passive-aggressive behaviour all day. He sits at home and makes messes and doesn't clean them and dishes out sass instead."

Later, I used Craigslist to email strangers with minivans offering their services as independent movers. I listened to music using noise-cancelling headphones, talked to no one except via email or internal chat messaging, toggled back and forth between work tasks and a browser tab with Facebook open in it.

"Were you offended when I tried speaking French to you the other day?" typed Shannon on Facebook Chat. "I worry about some things in my life."

"Not really," I typed. "I thought it was funny, you talking in French."

"I can speak French for real, though," typed Shannon. "Or at least better than that."

"I am a terrible employee," I typed. "Sometimes I think I can't possibly care less but then it happens again. I care less than I was caring."

"I know that feeling," typed Shannon. "Two years ago I worked at Fabricland during the summer. It was so underwhelming that it was almost overwhelming."

"In a meeting this morning, we talked about a pet game for smartphones by another company," I typed. "You tap balloons and then you tap pets and then the pets are happy and then it gives you more things to tap. It's a great success."

"Really?" typed Shannon.

"I think so," I typed. "They seem to be making a lot of money with it. When we brainstorm ideas here, there's always someone that's like, 'What would make a lot of money?' Then people say things like, 'The key in the dungeon,' or, 'Blocks falling down.' I always feel like saying, 'Dying alone,' just to see how people would react."

"Why do you even work there?" typed Shannon.

"I don't know," I typed. "I started in games when I was twenty-one. In Quebec City, people had serious jobs. I wanted to fit in. I thought things like, 'Put on hair products, it pleases people.' I really liked video games as a kid and didn't think I would outgrow them as an adult, but then I started being really unhappy and I blamed the unhappy on Quebec City and moved here. Not as many people have serious jobs here. Everyone's a DJ or something. Some people are more than one DJ. I have been feeling really burned out lately. I don't want a serious job anymore. I probably never even really wanted one."

"You should just quit," typed Shannon.

"I will," I typed. "I mean, the cost of living here is so low that there doesn't seem to be a point to it. Growing up, my parents were stressed about money. My dad yelled a lot. When I moved out, I think

I thought that if you ran out of money, you automatically starved to death. Maybe that's why I still haven't quit. But since moving here, I've been seeing people running out of money or owing a lot of money, but not stressing or starving to death. It's been eye-opening for me, I think. I am getting there."

"My dad is a business guy," typed Shannon. "It's his entire personality. When I was home for Christmas, he lectured me about my romantic life. He said I was open for business but running that business to the ground. He even makes business metaphors."

"My dad is angry inside," I typed, "but he also likes Zen koans and movies about escapades in foreign countries and unflavoured chips."

"Do you talk to your parents often?" typed Shannon.

"Not really," I typed. "In October, I talked to my mom on the phone. It was awkward. I told her I couldn't do video games anymore and wanted to reset my life and had started creative writing part-time, and she was like, what's wrong with video games? And why did you apply to an English university? She thought video games was a party career and that I would be doing that forever, so that didn't make sense to her at all. Then she said, 'As long as you're happy,' and I said, 'I wouldn't call it that.'"

"They don't miss you?" typed Shannon.

"I think they don't really want to be parents anymore," I typed. "They treat my sister the same way. They have more money now, so they buy expensive things and wait at home for the things to seem less interesting and then buy new things. They don't have friends and never see anyone or do anything. I think they're going feral, like wolf people. Soon they'll eat the dog. You can go feral and still live with a certain level of comfort. My parents are proving that."

"In high school, I did these talent shows," typed Shannon, "but my dad didn't want me to take singing lessons. He was afraid that all I would want to do after that was art. He was right."

In poetry class, we all had been assigned dates on which we would have to submit poems to the rest of the group for discussion. My poems had a kind of disaster quality to them, which I liked. They didn't rhyme or use poetic devices like enjambment, looked more like apologies than poems, which in a weird way seemed to make them even more into poems. At work, I had been designing video games based around mostly abstract concepts, like zombies or magic blocks or robots solving puzzles, so it felt good to be making something that was the complete opposite, close to me, personal, intimate. Through poems I submitted to class, I communicated things to people that I probably wouldn't have been able to tell them directly, wasn't even sure I had admitted to myself. What the poems were really saying was, "This shitty person that I am describing is me, but I don't want that person anymore. You can have it if you want, just take it." I felt like what had led me to poetry wasn't succeeding at life, but failing at it.

I imagined social services taking my self-esteem away from me, giving it to foster parents who would take better care of it.

The feeling that my life was going around in circles, and slightly faster each lap.

In the kitchen at work, I stood in line waiting to gain access to baskets of fresh fruits, which had been made available to all employees. Around me, small groups of men were socializing. Most of the men at the office were single and relied on their work environment to meet new people. With a ratio of maybe nine male employees to every female employee, they should have been sexually frustrated, forming street gangs roaming around town at night angrily smashing things, but somehow didn't seem to be. For the most part, people at work were nice and quiet and polite around others, as if completely devoid of sexual energy.

Just as I was exiting the metro station, I received a call on my phone. I didn't pick up, ignored the phone until it grew tired of asking, forcing the call to go to voicemail. Though I relied heavily on my phone, I rarely used it as a phone. I hated the sensation of conversing with an invisible person by shouting into a plastic case, felt more comfortable exchanging text messages.

Looking out the window, I saw that it was snowy and freezing and not a particularly good day to move. I thought, "Why would the universe go through all this trouble to create planets and physics and everything else, just to make the weather outside so shitty?" I ate a cereal bar and checked my phone for the time and saw that Greg the independent mover was late. I stared at my things, which formed a pile of nothing at the center of my room. There was a bed, two boxes of books, a small bookshelf, two small dressers, a blue lamp in the shape of a ghost, a black lamp in the shape of a lamp, clothes in garbage bags, other things in garbage bags, other boxes, other objects. I had been moving from apartment to apartment to apartment a lot, every time giving or throwing away things, shedding stuff the way an animal would shed a coat of fur. I could have bought new things to replace the old things, but then didn't. I now owned what seemed like so little that I couldn't get myself to buy anything anymore. Any attempt at shopping felt something like, "I can't buy these coasters, all I would own is these coasters, that would look ridiculous."

I felt like I was terrible at capitalism.

The doorbell rang. I walked to the front door and saw that Greg the independent mover had a normal body frame and not an overly muscular body frame. I had imagined Greg as a person with an overly muscular body frame and not a slim man in his early thirties wearing a plaid hat. Five minutes later, we began loading his vehicle. Coming up and down the stairs, we made small talk and then regular talk. Greg mentioned that he was trying to make it as an actor and that he was only moving people from time to time, as a quick way to make money. We double-teamed the bed. For my body, physical exercise felt like a question in some sort of made-up language. We struggled to get the bed down the stairs. Greg shouted, "We need more manpower!" and laughed. I didn't feel like the expression "manpower" applied to me.

In the minivan, we listened to talk radio. Greg made several driving mistakes, most of which involved underestimating the size of his vehicle.

"I still have no idea how to drive this thing," said Greg. "It's so funny. I only take the van when I move people. My wife is the one that uses it. I don't even own a car."

He laughed.

"It's like you're driving a hippo," I said.

"I know, right," he said. He smiled, seemed excited, childlike. I imagined taking him to a playground, watching him go down a blue plastic slide while I sat on a park bench and read a book, waiting for him to tire himself out.

"So you work in games. What do you do exactly?" said Greg.

"Game designer," I said.

"What does that do?" said Greg.

"I make a lot of flow charts," I said.

"Do you guys hire voice actors?" said Greg.

"Not really," I said. "We mostly make games for smartphones. Like Tetris."

"The blocks could have a voice," said Greg. "It's 2010! There's so much they can do now."

I unpacked boxes and things. Later, there still seemed to be the same number of boxes. Later, I grew tired of unpacking. My new room was the black hole roommate's old room. I had half-expected to open the door and find a room that looked like a crime scene, with busted walls, a broken window, a key-stabbed mattress, maybe purple graffiti that said "Ghostbusters." Instead, I had found a room that was empty and calm and clean-looking.

I sat on the couch in the common area and located the unprotected Wi-Fi signal. I thought about Ines saying, "It's a trap," and then imagined having to suddenly duck from poison darts or a giant boulder. I heard Niklas in his room talking in German on Skype with a person inside his laptop. He was the only one in the house, had said hi to me in an uncomfortable English accent before asking if I was the new roommate and then had specified that he lived here also. Two hours passed, somehow, and the passing of time allowed Ines and someone I hadn't met to return home.

"You're here," said Ines to me, smiling. She introduced me to Cristian, who had a short black moustache and was wearing a purple winter coat, a red tuque with matching gloves and an oversized sweater with a pale blue boat and a coconut tree on it. To gain access to his room, he had to force the door in with his shoulder a little. He threw his coat and other things anywhere and then closed the door.

"We went antique shopping today," said Cristian. "It was amazing. They had an old dining table from 1834. If I had the money, I would have bought everything."

"You keep saying that," said Ines. "But that's like the time you wanted to buy the fancy dinner plates. You would just be eating hot dogs off of them."

"Eating hot dogs," said Cristian, "like a king."

"Thomas, do you want to know what happened with Dan?" said Ines.

"That fucker," said Cristian.

"What happened?" I said.

"His last few days here," said Ines, "he had this look on his face, like you could tell that he was up to something. He was supposed to move out on the 31st but he ended up leaving during the night of the 29th. I don't know if you remember that night, but it was really cold. I went to bed around midnight and woke up freezing at five a.m. I was like, 'What the fuck?' I could hear water running from somewhere and there was no heat in the house. I got up and found the front door of the house wide open and then the hot and cold water taps in both the kitchen and the bathroom running at full capacity. I saw that Dan's bag and clothes were gone. I was like, 'That motherfucker.'"

"So, wait, he did that on purpose?" I said.

"Completely, one hundred percent on purpose," said Ines. "He just wanted to jack up our electricity bill, his little revenge on us for kicking him out. This won't affect you, though. We'll pay for it, but what a fucker."

Work was a no-emotion zone for me, a place where I disconnected from pleasure entirely. On most days, coming out, I felt exhausted, even though all I had done was sit in a comfortable chair and stare at a source of light for several hours. I knew I was going to find the willpower to quit at some point, maybe even soon, but until then, my plan was to survive by being as asocial as possible, removing myself mentally from the office, sealing myself far and away in my brain. If video games were "escapist fantasies," then what I was doing felt like escapism from escapism, some meta form of escapism.

Even if I was consciously trying to avoid socializing at work, Ana sometimes got me to go out for lunch with her and other people. Ana was an illustrator who had been hired around the same time as me and had recently announced that she would be leaving the company at the end of the month. The entire time I had courted her, she hadn't figured out that I was courting her. At some point, she had introduced me to her friend Mason, who wore polo shirts and was self-confident and cheerful and didn't seem to view his own existence as some sort of perplexing burden. Then she had started seeing Mason and we had stopped hanging out outside of work. What hurt a little was knowing that choosing him over me had probably been a good decision on her end.

At the soup place, I wanted to sit near her but ended up at the other end of the table, next to Sebastian, who was also a game designer.

"This is what bothers me," said Sebastian. "Barrels. It's always barrels. They're in every single game. I have probably destroyed a million video game barrels in my life. Here's the thing: Have you ever tried kicking down a barrel, in real life? They're pretty much indestructible."

One of the reasons why I didn't want to talk to people at work anymore was that conversations were almost always about video games. I had stopped playing video games more or less completely, because in general I had begun to feel as if they were still taking something from me, but no longer giving back. Despite this, I probably knew more about Sebastian's views on modern first-person shooters than I knew about him. This seemed strange in comparison to people from school, like Shannon, who talked about personal things a lot and had a blog and liked bluntly emotional novels and was so used to writing and sharing her feelings that it felt like she was, at all times, on the verge of making a confession.

"Brittany," read the fridge magnet guarding a postcard from Brent that had arrived by mail. It was my third day at the house. "Hi guys, I am in Guatemala," read a note from Brent on the back of the card. On the front was an alien vessel firing red beams at a Mayan temple. I imagined an alien sitting at a desk like mine from work, hating his job, feeling numb, firing red beams at the temple, feeling more numb. "Endurance," I thought.

I heard Cristian coming out of his room. He had slept for most of the day. In comparison, I had awoken around eight-thirty a.m., metroed to work, done nothing fascinating there, come back.

It felt like both our days were about to begin.

"I am the opposite of a farmer," said Cristian. "It's six p.m. and I just got up."

He powered up my Xbox 360 and then sat down on the couch in the common area. I went to the bathroom, locked myself in, turned on both water taps, undressed, stepped in the shower. I stood under the shower head and waited as water fell on me. The universe was a harsh place, which was why I enjoyed taking hot showers. I applied shampoo and then petted my own head to distribute the shampoo evenly. I thought about school, having peers who were five or six or seven years younger than me, how strange it felt to hear them say things like, "I was supposed to do this essay but then I ended up taking pictures of my leg." Going back to school after having a serious job for a few years was making me feel like I was doing my twenties in reverse.

For no specific reason, I looked up and then spotted something I hadn't noticed before: a plastic machine gun resting on a small ledge above the shower head. Staring at the object, my face became more complex and then less complex. A few minutes later, I dried myself using a beach towel. I thought about how this beach towel had never seen the beach. Coming out, I saw that Ines was now making chili, which looked like beans and the colour red. Cristian was drinking apple juice from a mug with rainforest animals on it and playing a video game on the small television monitor. In the video game, a vampire slayer was killing vampires in a vampire lair.

"I hadn't noticed the machine gun in the shower until now," I said. I sat on the couch next to Cristian.

"Oh yeah, that's from last Halloween," said Cristian. "Ines bought that for her costume. We put it there the next day, I don't remember why. It just stayed there."

"I like it," I said.

"I am going to be such a good mom," said Ines. She turned towards us, holding a small bowl with chili in it. "Look at this."

"It looks beautiful," said Cristian. I didn't say anything. I didn't understand the point of making food aesthetically pleasing, felt vaguely alienated from the beautiful food.

"I know, right?" said Ines.

"Oh, wait," said Cristian. "I forgot. I downloaded new music when I was at my mom's house the other night. Hold on."

Cristian got up, went to his room, returned with an old iPod. He plugged the device into portable computer speakers and browsed the music library. The iPod emitted little clicks. Cristian selected an album and then sat back on the couch. A song began playing, the disco version of a classic *Star Wars* song.

"This is crazy," said Christian. He laughed. "It's an entire album of that."

"Where did you find this?" I said.

"Music forums," said Cristian. "I don't have a computer here and I hate talking to my mom, so whenever I am at her house, I just use her computer a lot. I can spend hours downloading music or reading articles on Wikipedia. Like, what's rice? Why does it expand when you put in water? Why would evolution give us rice? What was its purpose in nature? I love that stuff."

"So your mom lives around here," I said.

"Hochelaga," said Cristian. "My dad moved back to Argentina."

"I saw Laura on the street today," said Ines. "She looked so lost without Brent."

"Why did he go to South America?" I said. "Brent, I mean."

"He's from Australia," said Ines. "Last winter was his first year in Montreal. His skin was used to getting a lot of sunlight and he started getting all these weird plaques on his arms and legs. At one point, he even had to go to a tanning salon. This year, I think his brother was going to be in South America, so they decided to meet there. I don't think they're that close, though. It was mostly just to avoid spending the winter here."

"Do you remember the time he slept under a car?" said Cristian.

"I know," said Ines. "I was thinking about that the other day. That was so funny. Poor baby. He was too drunk. He didn't know where he was. He just slept there."

"I told that story to Kyle last night," said Cristian. "I was surprised he didn't know it."

"So you ended up going out last night?" I said.

"Yeah," said Cristian. "Kyle had a friend in town. I wanted to meet his friend."

"I thought you said you wanted to stay in," I said.

"I did, I was really tired," said Cristian, "but I don't know, I pulled through. I am invincible. I am this guy."

He pointed at the screen. In the video game, the vampire slayer was slaying a vampire using elaborate decapitation techniques.

"I need the magic boots but they're impossible to get," said Cristian. "They're on the other side, across that gap there. I can't make the jump."

"That's a good metaphor for desire," I said. "You want the thing but there's a gap between you and the thing. And you can see the thing, it's right there. But you can't get to it."

"Right," said Cristian. "Because I don't have the magic boots."

"No," I said. "I mean, never mind."

I googled Brent by his full name and found his Twitter account and then an interview with him by a local blog. Ines had told me that the house screened movies from time to time, but reading the article, I learned that we actually operated, during the summer, a "free weekly underground cinema called Cinedrome" that drew about a hundred and twenty attendees per screening. "Rooftop cinemas are fairly common in Australia, but they're less so here," said Brent in the interview. "That's where the inspiration came from. There's a lot of complications with running Cinedrome in our backyard, with neighbours and all kinds of things that can and do go wrong. On the other hand, people that come to our screenings sometimes lose sunglasses or lighters or whatever, and we find them the next day and usually get to keep them. It's a real gold mine."

Constantly on the computer, constantly producing content, constantly going nowhere.

Repeatedly not having sex felt like a kind of abuse.

Smoking outside with Shannon before class, she referred to Patricia as a "mom," which surprised me. In general, when I didn't know someone in my poetry class's age, I usually assigned that person an imaginary number in my head, only to find out later that my estimate was higher than the actual number. The only person who this system didn't apply to was Patricia, who, for some reason, frequently and casually referenced her age, two years older than me, aloud during discussions. What surprised me wasn't so much Shannon's frank assessment of Patricia, but becoming fully aware that she felt an age difference with Patricia, but not with me.

Walking down the street, I was talking to myself because I had things to tell me.

I asked the coffee machine to give me hot water for tea and then the gears inside it made noises. The machine screamed at me for about twenty seconds. It was Monday. Negative feelings were ejaculating all over my frontal lobes while tired blood was passing through my body as if enduring a boring amusement park ride. Every week felt like a botched copy-paste of the week before it, work for five consecutive days and then a pause of two days and then that same dream-nightmare all over again. I never felt rested from the pause, just dizzy from all the start-and-stop.

In front of me were wall-mounted television monitors displaying video trailers of video games the studio had published. Our titles were polished and nice to look at, but also weirdly hollow and artless, as if made by all the beautiful but vapid people on television or in movies. From a side angle, I saw Julian, who managed the design department, walk to the sink to wash his water bottle. I thought, "Please don't talk to me." Julian was a bored dad in his early forties trapped at some unclear level of what seemed like an infinite corporate hierarchy. Other people at work were bored dads or future bored dads. Julian wasn't someone I admired or looked up to, just a person I felt I would eventually turn into if I did nothing, stayed where I was, waited long enough.

Julian asked about my weekend and I thought, "Shit," and replied, "Good, how was yours?" I knew we were going to make small talk or discuss video games, which was possibly worse than small talk. I tried to come up with an excuse to escape the conversation and imagined the aliens on Brent's postcard randomly choosing this moment to fire red beams at the office, which didn't help. Julian said that he had spent most of his weekend playing Bioshock II. In the video game, a person with a giant drill and magic powers goes looking for a child in an underwater city enduring an armed conflict. Julian described at length and even physically reenacted one of the action sequences for me.

Later, I sat at my desk and began updating a game design document. The purpose of the document was for artists and programmers and producers to read the file and understand what they were working on without having to talk to each other or me. It was an interesting definition of teamwork. I was working on a new version of Scrabble for iPhone. The year before, the studio had released a version of Scrabble for lower-end phones. Because someone had decided that we would be recycling most of the programming code and game mechanics from that title, I barely had to think of things for this project. So far, I had come up with only one real idea, which was to organize the Create Game menus and sub-menus in a manner that would evoke sitting down around a table before playing a board game.

"I am reading my text messages from last night in backward order," typed Shannon on Facebook Chat. "It's like being on the wrong end of the movie *Memento*. I texted so much shit."

"What did you do?" I typed.

"Stereo is such a sketchy place," typed Shannon. "Older guys in the back doing enough cocaine to kill a three-year-old. What fucking monster comes out of me when I am partying? I am an embarrassment. I should just cage myself in my room."

"It probably wasn't as bad as you think it was," I typed.

"Sometimes it feels like this city is going to kill me, and like that can't happen soon enough," typed Shannon.

"What happened?" I typed.

"All these things," Shannon typed. "At the end, it was just me and these two chicks I sort of know. We were bored, and one of them told the other, 'You never wear makeup, I want to see you wearing makeup,' and I knew it was a bad idea but I didn't feel like objecting to anything anymore. She put makeup on her friend and I think she wanted her to look pretty, but she just looked psychotic. Then later we listened to aggressive music at a low volume and I fell asleep on someone's couch. I feel surprisingly awake for some reason right now. Maybe I am still fucked."

I didn't type anything for a few minutes.

"Am I over-sharing?" typed Shannon.

"No, I am just tabbing a lot," I typed. "I am still at work, so I am mildly distracted by work."

"Oh, right," typed Shannon. "Work."

Growing up, I spent a lot of time playing Sim City. Too much, probably. Later in life, I realized that I really liked cities, that what I wanted, at all times, was a floor above the one I was currently on, higher skyscrapers, even more confusing malls.

There was no meaning to human life and the only thing I could do about that was to search Google for "Coping with absence."

Niklas was used to partying pretty hard. Because clubs in Germany closed later than bars in Canada, he sometimes came home at three a.m., drunk but not tired enough to go to bed, and then swept floors or cleaned things for a while to kill time, tire himself out. We all liked this and found this very useful, but we also knew that Niklas would be going back home soon, which meant we would have to come up with an entirely new strategy to keep the house tidy.

I was making more money than I was spending. There was money in my bank account, but I didn't seem interested in spending it on anything. I liked it there, in my bank account, waiting.

But here's the thing: Maybe I didn't want to live in a city so much as observe one from a close distance, like in Sim City. Living in a city was like living multiple lives, each capable of crushing me. It meant forcing myself to meet people, impenetrable three-dimensional emotion factories, being nice to them because I never knew what being nice to them could lead to, parties to attend or job opportunities or collaborating on something or whatever else. The insane number of possibilities a city offered. Trying to compute that number in my head felt like a kind of string theory.

Waiting for the Wi-Fi signal to reappear, I sat in the common area and read *Et Tu, Babe* by Mark Leyner. In the book, a writer achieves an unsustainable level of fame and fortune, causing his self-destruction. We were stealing internet access from a random neighbour, which meant we had no control over the router. Sometimes the Wi-Fi signal went rogue, vanished. Not having internet access didn't feel like life before the internet era, it felt like a kind of dire alternate reality in which everyone had internet access but me. Without the internet, reality felt hollow, like a room without furniture. It wasn't crammed with infinity YouTubes, or the never-ending thoughts and obsessions of human people who refreshingly weren't me.

About forty minutes passed. Someone knocked on the front door. I put the book down, made a face, didn't expect knocking.

"Cristian?" said a man in maybe his sixties as I opened the door. His eyebrows were massive, as if several eyebrows stacked on top of one another. He was overweight, had a belly coming out of him like it was trying to unmerge from him, live independently from him, once there gain perspective maybe, yearn to go back.

"No," I said.

"You're not Cristian," said the man.

"No," I said, "I just moved in."

"Are Cristian or Ines here?" said the man.

"They're not," I said.

"Okay," said the man. "I am Pierre. I own the building. I need the rent. Before, when Brittany was here, it was okay, I would get it on time. But you guys have been really sloppy lately. We're past mid-February. I still don't have it."

"Ines handles the rent," I said in French. I assumed that Pierre was French Canadian and that he would prefer not having to con-verse with me in English. "I gave her my share. I'll text her about this right now."

"Can I come in?" said Pierre in French.

"Sure," I said.

Pierre walked in, examined the common area, kitchen, backyard, made heavy breathing noises while doing so, as if his organs were solidifying, becoming rock-like, like molten lava. He seemed tense and apprehensive and made remarks about Cristian's room, the floor of which wasn't even visible. Before leaving, he asked for my full name and phone number, which I wrote down on a piece of paper for him. It was only then we realized that his last name and my last name were the same last name. Though I was pretty sure we weren't related, Pierre seemed to enjoy thinking we were. He began smiling more and suddenly seemed more relaxed.

"I'd like to deal with you from now on," said Pierre.

"The golden days of Brittany," said Ines, four hours later. "That's funny. Did he really say that? It was ten times worse when Brittany was doing rent. Sometimes they would just scream at each other, like the goal wasn't even to make sense, the goal was just to out-scream the other person. Pierre likes to give us shit because we did the screenings last summer without telling him. When he found out, he wanted us to stop immediately because he was afraid something would happen to the building. I took care of rent, though. It's in the mail. It just took longer this month because of Cristian. He's always either broke or really broke."

At Blizzarts, I bought Shannon a beer. Later, she said, "Let's find you a girl," and added that "It would be funny." She asked me what my type was and I said, "I don't know," and then, "American Apparel chick," and she said, "That could be anyone," and I said, "I guess."

My approach with women was like stacking blocks really high in Tetris while waiting for a straight line that might never come.

Impractical desires that fall apart when introduced to concrete reality.

I received a Facebook message from someone named Romy Nelson. The message said that we didn't know each other but that she was also studying creative writing and that our common friend Shannon had shown her a poem by me and that she would like to publish it in her zine, which was small and not serious and had no goal other than existing. "Probably the deadline is March 1st," read one of the message's final lines. I replied positive things to Romy and added her as a friend and then stalked her Facebook account a little.

The subtext of the internet: You are alone.

At work, I could go days without thinking anything but basic mental operations, like two plus five equals seven.

"At least, people at your job, they hate it," I said to Cristian. "They want to get out. They bond over that."

My plan was to follow my phone like a treasure map, but then I couldn't find the loft and had to text back and forth with Cristian. His text messages were all short, imprecise, felt more like clues than facts, like being given directions by someone out of breath. My phone's ringtone for text messages was the default ringtone, little beeps, and sounded like what I would imagine a car bomb about to go off would sound like. By the time I found the loft, many car bombs had gone off.

From outside, party music sounded like kazoo music. Walking up, I saw people smoking, talking on the sidewalk. I had interacted with more or less no one that day and became aware that going any farther would mean having to switch to social mode, exist around people, flawed people, random and estranged from themselves, impulsive both consciously and unconsciously, a kind of stir-fry mix of personality traits. I hesitated before going in. The thought of graduating to any state other than boredom seemed anxiety-causing. I wasn't sure what I was doing there, if I would feel like I belonged or just end up alone in a crowd of assholes. I imagined myself turning around, going back home, feeling both relieved and ashamed, binge-eating cereal, hiding in my room, doing internet things, feeling in control again.

I compromised with myself by entering the space looking for an excuse to give up. Inside were about thirty or forty people. If I wasn't the oldest in that group, then I was close. I scouted the room and felt like my anxiety was trying to give me contextual advice, like a computer-controlled sidekick in a video game. I didn't realize that I was staring at a small group until the small group decided to move. I thought, "To stare at people until they go away is what a cat would do." I spotted Cristian in the back, drinking a beer and dancing without dancing. He was wearing a t-shirt that said

"Graphic" and had a lion on it. He looked like "an awesome guy trying to figure out life."

"Where's Niklas?" I said, after saying hey and then unimportant things.

"He's somewhere," said Cristian. "I don't know where. This is Kyle, by the way."

"Hi," I said.

"Hi," said Kyle. He smiled. He had no facial hair, was wearing chino pants and a plaid shirt that looked like a sliding tile puzzle. "Wait, what's your name?"

"Thomas," I said. "I am Cristian's new roommate. This is our other roommate's unofficial goodbye thing."

"Oh, that's you," said Kyle. "Cristian mentioned you. I didn't know that was you."

"Hold on," said Cristian. "I'll be right back."

Kyle and I stared at each other. When meeting people, I always felt like I started at negative something. I was a guy, and not an interesting looking one, and generally assumed that the person I was talking to was jaded about meeting new people. I felt like I needed to say redeeming things about myself or my life, present myself as a kind of magic trick that would wow the person and maybe astonish the person, because otherwise I would be just another human in a city that received fresh injections of new bodies to meet on a weekly basis. What was even more terrifying than interviewing people was being interviewed by them, being asked things like, "What do you do?" and, "Where are you from?" and then, while answering, observing them trying to decide whether they wanted to keep me or else saw no use for me, felt bad for me a little, wanted, on some level, to put me out of my misery. Meeting people often led to this anxiety, this massive, complicated, exhausting anxiety of, "Am I impressing you now, are you satisfied with me, shouldn't we be talking about bands by now?" It kept things unpredictable.

"So how's life at that house?" said Kyle.

"It's good," I said. "Everyone was so nice to me the first week I was there. I think they were just happy I wasn't Dan. How do you know Cristian?"

"Just, from around," said Kyle. "Did you know him before moving in?"

"No, I was from Craigslist," I said, as if Craigslist was my place of birth.

"I was from Craigslist too, when I moved into my place," said Kyle. "Is Cristian still reading his mystery novel? He was reading this book a few weeks ago, trying to figure who the killer was. He was really into it, but then he just stopped talking about it. I don't know if he dropped it."

"Maybe he was traumatized by who the killer was and doesn't want to talk about it anymore," I said.

I meant that last sentence as a joke, but Kyle failed to react, so we both stared at each other again. I thought, "I am not drunk enough to talk to people." From a medium distance, I saw Shannon walking in and then removing her coat and winter things. She was wearing a dark blue dress and torn leggings. I waved at her calmly.

"Baby," said Shannon, excited, hugging me a little. "Have you been here long? Have the bands started?"

"I got here maybe fifteen minutes ago," I said. "I think only one band played. There's another setting up now. This is Kyle."

Kyle and Shannon said hi to each other.

"How's your life?" I said to Shannon.

"I am kind of messy," said Shannon. "It was my last session with my therapist today. Last night, nothing bad happened, I just met this guy and we talked at his place and then went to his friend's opening. I wanted to keep talking to him, so we sat in a corner and ignored everyone. Then back at his place, we split a pill of MDMA and had the rawest conversation, like nothing off limits. Then we hooked up. I don't know if he'll call me back."

"I think we've met before," said Kyle.

"I was just going to say that, you look really familiar," said Shannon. "But then I am so used to seeing the same faces everywhere I go. Sometimes I don't even know these people. I just know their faces."

"Yeah," I said. "It's like, there's these people on Facebook I've never met, but then I see their profiles all the time attending things I want to go to, so I kind of know them from that, and if I see them in public, it's always weird, like I don't think of them as people, I think of them as characters, like characters from a sitcom."

"Characters from Facebook," said Shannon. She laughed.

"Exactly," I said. "I wanted to ask you, do you know who Romy Nelson is? You know her, right?"

"I know her," said Shannon. "I like her. I saw her at Sparrow on Tuesday. Why?"

"I haven't met her, we just talked by email," I said.

"I think she might come here tonight," said Shannon. "I'll introduce you guys."

"Oh, good," I said. "Thank you."

I heard a guitar making sounds and then a keyboard making different sounds. I turned around. In the back of the loft, two or three people appeared ready to play. There was no stage, only a little area with music equipment and what looked like a maze of wires. "Hey, you guys," said someone in the only mic. The band was a local band whose name was a normal word spelled without vowels. Lacking vowels was good. I went to the makeshift bar and purchased a beer and then went through the crowd and found Cristian. Next to him was Niklas, who was visibly drunk and emotional about having to leave Montreal and being overly affectionate, kissing people on their heads like they were newborns. "I am going to miss you guys," he said, while hugging two people I didn't know. I wanted him to be drunk. I wanted him to be drunk and kissing people on their heads like they were newborns. I wanted him to be drunk and kissing people like they were newborns and for the people to feel cared for and less alone afterwards.

Niklas hugged me and then kissed me on the head like a newborn.

The band's first song was about the moonlight and the feeling of finding yourself under it. The band's second song was about the continent of Africa. I tried to imagine how people living in Africa would react to the song called "Africa." I checked my phone for the time and thought about having to leave because of work the next day. Then I thought, "Fuck it." I stayed. The vowel band played and then another band played. I drank more beers, smoked maybe a third of Cristian's cigarette, got excited, moshed, pushed people and then was pushed by other people, felt good, didn't care about my body anymore. After the second band's set, Cristian introduced me to JJ, who had black hair and a small lip ring and was wearing a dark gray hoodie. Through conversation, I picked up that JJ sold drugs on the side. A few minutes later, I purchased MDMA from him. Upon completing the exchange, JJ said, "Thank you very much" politely, and I said, "You're welcome." I only did drugs occasionally, didn't have a dealer, or maybe arbitrariness was my dealer. I was good with addictions, could smoke cigarettes or do drugs without getting hooked or feeling the need for them the next day.

On my way to the bathroom, I felt disoriented a little. The room was moving around, getting away from me, coming back, as if homesick. To be drunk was to be more acutely aware that I was living on a giant planet and that the giant planet was itself in motion. I realized that my arms and face were covered in sweat. I thought, "Too drunk to notice the heat." I found an empty bathroom stall with a door that didn't close. I transferred the MDMA from the little plastic bag JJ had given me to a gastric bag inside my body. I wanted to get whatever part of my brain that usually thinks, "I give up," to give up. What I was doing in the stall was obvious to anyone passing by. No one seemed to care and I felt vaguely self-conscious.

Then I went back into the crowd.

Then I drank more beers for no reason other than because I could.

Then, talking to Shannon, I began to feel good and alive and conversation-worthy.

Then a DJ played party songs about partying from his MacBook and I tried dancing but wasn't sure if the dancing was making me feel outstanding or demented or both.

Then I felt a little bit like the universe, a vast mass of energy, open, ever-changing, ever-evolving, harmony within chaos, many paradoxes.

Then Shannon was drunk and fell into a small table and knocked all the beer bottles on it to the ground.

Then she made out with a guy wearing a flannel shirt and it made me visualize her sex drive as a fancy car from a car commercial crashing into a brick wall at maximum speed.

Then I had a conversation with someone I didn't know and I said, "What do you do?" and she said, "I don't know," and then added, "That's probably not a very original answer," and I said, "No, that's a very original answer," and we both laughed nervously.

Then I gave up talking to her.

Then I visualized my own sex drive as a merry-go-round, cute horses bobbing up and down gently for a few minutes and then stopping.

Then I didn't care anymore and left shortly after without saying anything to anyone.

I felt like I was married to the word "Never."

I had slept fully dressed, with a jacket and things scattered around me in the bed. I got up and saw that my phone was making existential noises. I had a new voicemail. It was two in the afternoon. I went to the kitchen and drank water. No one was home. I had a headache and could hear in the back of my head a kind of crackling, like the sound a campfire makes. I had missed work, but hadn't told anyone that I wouldn't be showing up. I thought about this and felt bad, but then not really. I opened Google Chrome and began composing an email and could only come up with uninspired excuses to explain my absence. I wrote something about being sick and pressed the Send button. I imagined being caught lying and getting fired, but the thought seemed more calming than alarming.

I drank water again and then circled around the same seven websites for about two hours. Going from party mode to waking up alone in a silent apartment seemed depressing. I made Facebook more interesting by adding people I had met the night before. I thought, "The goal of life is to make Facebook more interesting." I found JJ, whose real name was Jeffrey. Staring at his number of friends, I thought, "I should be a drug dealer, just to have a lot of Facebook friends."

"Where did you go last night?" typed Shannon on Facebook Chat. "You disappeared at some point."

"I just left," I typed. "Sorry I didn't say goodbye. I didn't think you would care."

"I didn't," typed Shannon. "It's not a big deal. Did you see Romy?"

"Was she there?" I typed.

"She was," typed Shannon, "but I don't think she stayed for more than an hour. She didn't know anyone."

"Shit," I typed.

"There was this girl last night," typed Shannon. "Lindsey. She kept telling me she envies my freedom. I was like, 'What freedom?' I fuck dumb guys to justify my contempt for men. That's not freedom."

"I get what she means, though," I typed. "She probably only knows party you. Regular you is more reserved. It's funny, when you added me on Facebook, I was like, 'Oh, shy girl that sits in the back of the class and never says anything, okay.' Then I looked at your profile and stared at your number of friends and didn't understand how you had that many. It started to make sense when I saw that you had a Tumblr with poems and party photos of you and pictures of pretty rocks on it."

"I just hate talking in class," typed Shannon. "Everyone is staring at me, it's too much pressure. I do better with the night crowd. Everyone's drunk. I don't have to make sense. All I have to do is want something."

"You're good at that," I typed. "A party inspiration for everyone else."

"Great," typed Shannon.

"I didn't mean that negatively," I typed.

I couldn't get myself to think of Shannon in sexual terms, as someone available to me.

"Are you feeling better today?" said Julian. I was.

As employees, we were given "shares," which I never bothered looking into. I didn't know if I owned shares or was expected to buy shares or if collecting enough shares would give me the power to fire myself. I had ignored multiple emails about the shares and then received one that was flagged and said "IMPORTANT" in all caps and seemed angry at me. The email wanted me to click on a link and then enter personal information to accept my shares, which I didn't know I needed to do. I felt like I was being bullied into being given company shares.

I went out with Cristian and Kyle for three nights in a row, from Tuesday to Thursday. The default script for going out was to pre-drink at the house and then head to wherever it was we were going a little after midnight. It didn't matter what we were going to. It could have been a baptism and we would still have showed up only after midnight. On all three nights, Cristian and Kyle were trolling for girls. I didn't know what I was trolling for, maybe just a hangover. On the first and second night, I got bored around two a.m. and felt sufficiently drunk and didn't think that I was needed anymore. I left without telling them, to avoid them trying to convince me to stay. On the third night, Cristian met a girl and for some reason began talking to her about astrophysics, telling her he had read on Wikipedia that outer space emitted a loud noise at an inaudible frequency and so that the universe was essentially screaming at us at all times. Somehow, he later came home with her.

Ines had been working on two paintings in her room. One of the paintings was of Ellen DeGeneres in 1994 looking satanic and the other was of Ellen DeGeneres in 1998 looking satanic. It was the second week of March and a Saturday. I sat in the common area and replied to a Facebook message from Romy whose first line read, "I am sorry I've been so 2007 with my response quickness." Romy was never on Chat and so we mostly used Facebook as a kind of deluxe email system. Ines came out of her room, went to the fridge, poured orange juice into a wine glass. We didn't own normal glasses, just wine glasses and assorted mugs. About a minute later, Cristian returned home.

"Were you okay this morning?" said Ines.

"What?" said Cristian.

"That was so funny," said Ines. "You came out of your room half-asleep. You had, like, one shoe on and the other foot was barefoot. Then you realized you were late for work, so you looked surprised, put on clothes and then ran out the door."

"My alarm clock never went off," said Cristian. "Or maybe it went off and I just wanted to sleep more. But it was fine. I have tricks. As long as the assistant manager doesn't see me coming in, I don't get yelled at. He just thinks I've been working downstairs."

"As long as you're okay," said Ines. "Did I tell you guys that Brent will be back on the 25th? I am so excited to see him! Also, the electric bill came in yesterday and it's pretty messed up. The font they used looks more bold than the normal bold. I don't know how we're going to pay all of that."

"We'll figure it out," said Cristian. "Maybe we could have a garage sale."

"I don't know what we could sell," said Ines. "If we had a garage sale, it would just depress people. They would give us things."

On Facebook, I posted something about being at the Concordia University library and then a minute later, Romy added a comment that read, "I'll come find you," but she never did.

"Enchanté," said some other girl Cristian had come home with. Sometimes, because of my French accent betraying me, people liked to say "Enchanté" instead of "Nice to meet you" when meeting me, which they thought was polite, but also made them sound like demented magicians a little.

In his email, which was addressed to Cristian, Ines and me, Niklas explained that he was back home and well, but that he still "dreamt in English and in Canada."

I didn't do anything on my birthday. I stayed home, sat in the common area, read *Herzog* by Saul Bellow. In the book, a confused intellectual man struggles to come to terms with the general failure of his life.

"It's your birthday," said Ines an hour later, smiling. She had already wished me a happy birthday on Facebook. "How old are you?"

"Twenty-six," I said. This was a lie. In reality, I was turning twenty-seven, but felt so used to saying twenty-six that I failed to correct myself. Then it dawned on me that I hadn't revealed my exact age to anyone in the house and that my birth year wasn't listed on Facebook.

Saying twenty-six now felt good in comparison to my actual age.

To age was to think, "I am awesome," and then, "No, wait," and then a long list of reasons why you're not, with the list getting longer and longer each year.

I saw on Facebook that Romy was showcasing her zine at a thing and so decided to stop by. Walking around, I found the zine, but not her. My poem was on page seven and looked good next to a drawing of a skull giving another skull life advice.

One thing I knew about myself was that I definitely wasn't a hedonist. I didn't like things, experienced most of reality at the brain level, thought of my body as more of a holding cell than a temple of pleasure.

Brent had left a voicemail on Cristian's phone mentioning that he was back and would come by the house the next day. The voicemail was two minutes of him talking and then twenty minutes of Laura and her little sister playing a board game and not realizing they were being recorded.

The more I thought about it, the more I felt like my age was a number that represented how bad I felt about my age.

I was introduced to Brent, who asked me if I was "the new guy." I said yes and he replied, "Cool," in a neutral tone and then abruptly moved on to something else. Brent had excellent hair, was a natural leader, liked to say things like, "I am shooting a video with this person," or, "I am working on a new project with this other person." He kept himself busy, wasn't around a lot, but then talked loudly when he was, as if to compensate.

Eating alone in front of my laptop.

YouTube video suggestion: "Cute lemur enjoys rice."

Staring at the microwave, I made a face and then a second face. The microwave was a newer model and not our microwave. I opened the door leading to the backyard and stepped outside. I stretched.

In a nearby alley, there was a cat fighting a cat that was fighting another cat. It was early April. Up until that week, it had been a vintage winter, cold, hopeless, as if copy-pasted from 1994, or some other year desperate to make a comeback. Then the weather had experienced some sort of glitch, giving us six consecutive days of random sun. From having been cut off for several months, it felt like people were craving the sun, going outside, to the park, to the mountain, reclaiming the streets, prematurely wearing cut-off shorts, t-shirts, eating popsicles, ice-cream bars, soup best served cold. The backyard didn't have snow in it anymore, was dirty and grassless and looked like a practice space for mini-bikes. Brent was cleaning the space while listening to complex techno music. He had started a fire in a metal trash can, was burning tree branches and leaves and remnants from the year before, like half-decomposed boxes of Pabst Blue Ribbon.

Around four p.m., he banged on Cristian's door to wake him up.

"Cristian," said Brent. "I emptied the shed and made a pile of all your shit. You're allowed to keep three objects from the pile. I am throwing the rest out."

There was a short delay and then Cristian came out of his room, wanted to protest a little but was interrupted before being able to get a sentence going.

"Come on, man," said Brent. "It's junk. You don't need junk. If I don't make you throw it out, you'll just want to keep everything."

"Hold on," said Cristian. "Give me ten minutes."

Forty-five minutes later, Cristian was sorting through the pile while smoking a cigarette. Brent was now kicking a soccer ball around.

"Laura is coming over later with her friends," said Brent. "They haven't seen me since I got back, so they want to see me. We're all going out after, I think. You should come with us."

"I have to meet Kyle soon, but I'll be back later," said Cristian.

"Good," said Brent.

"We stole that microwave last night," said Cristian.

"Ines was asking about that," said Brent.

"Where is she?" said Cristian.

"I think she's at school," said Brent. "Where did you get the microwave from?"

"There's a basement apartment down the street, I don't know if you saw it," said Cristian. "Someone smashed their window a few days ago and no one repaired it, so I don't think anyone lives there right now. Last night, I was walking back home with Kyle and we were drunk. I thought it would be funny if I went in there and did a little dance, but then I got in and saw the microwave. Ours was getting really disgusting, so I just took theirs. It's almost new."

"Wait, did you come home directly?" said Brent.

"Yeah, but it was dark and there was no one outside," said Cristian.

"You can't do that," said Brent. "It's right down the street. Some-one could have seen you. They could have called the cops. If you're going to steal something, do it right. Don't come home directly, dump it somewhere, go get it the next day."

"You're right, that was dumb," said Cristian. "It seemed like a good idea. Then it wasn't."

"It's okay," said Brent. "If no one says anything, we'll just keep it, I guess. Thank you."

"You're welcome," said Cristian.

Brent's attention shifted to a wooden basement door near the shed. The door presumably led underneath the building, had a small lock on it, was fractured in multiple places. By kicking it a few times, Brent was able to break the door slightly, allowing him to remove the lock.

"What are you doing?" said Cristian.

"Pierre is going to have to buy a new one," said Brent. "I just want to see what's down there."

I walked towards Brent to help him open the door. "Thanks,"

said Brent, his hands dirty. Behind the door were gray steps that led underneath the building. Brent descended the stairs, disappeared, was followed by me, then Cristian. We looked around for a few minutes. Under the building was nothing interesting, just spiderwebs, dirt. I imagined the low ceiling coming down on us, crushing our bodies, transforming them into paste. "It's a trap," I thought. "Set by whoever has free Wi-Fi." We re-emerged above ground, closing the door behind us. "We can use this space," said Brent. "I don't know for what, but we can use it."

About an hour passed. Brent introduced me to Laura, his girl-friend. She was wearing an oversized tee with a pocket on the left side, and a short skirt with dots on it. I went to the bathroom and spent an unknown amount of time applying hair product, trying to come up with a combination of face and hair that made aesthetic sense. No combination seemed entirely satisfying. I heard strangers coming in. I applied more hair product, which accomplished nothing. "Thomas, come meet attractive women," I heard Brent yell. It felt like even if I managed to get my hair in a position I could live with, it would immediately rebel against me, self-destruct, revert to making me look dumb.

I thought, "I wish I was a torso and that's it."

Coming out, I saw that Laura and her friend were making quinoa salad and other salads. Laura introduced me to her friend, who was named Jeremy. In the backyard, Brent was lighting dollar-store candles while talking to people I couldn't see.

"Brent, are you really wearing this?" said Laura.

"It's hot, what else do you want me to wear?" said Brent. "You should get used to it. I'll be wearing this wife-beater all summer. Maybe I'll even start beating you."

"I'll beat you," mumbled Laura.

Several minutes later, Brent, Laura, their friends and I sat down on an old blanket outside, began drinking, eating. For the most part, I sat there, observed people, participated minimally. Brent took over the conversation and began telling everyone a story from the summer before, about Cristian doing mushrooms for the first time, eating too many, then them getting separated that night, with Brent coming back home around six a.m. and finding Cristian in the backyard staring at the sunrise, crying a little and softly repeating, "It's so beautiful," over and over again.

Laura was smoking a cigarette and sharing it with the girl sitting next to her, who was wearing a shirt with garden gnomes on it and who I was pretty sure was named Mira. I asked for a drag, which was just a cheap ploy to talk to Laura's friend. I wanted to talk to Mira. I wanted to tell Mira about myself. I wanted to tell Mira, "I have low self-esteem and my sex life probably has abandonment issues by now and I feel very cynical about my capacity to have a stable relationship and not fuck up or grow to loathe myself within the relationship, though maybe all I want on some level is just to be proven wrong." I was introduced to Mira and was told that Mira's name was Mira and that she studied studio arts at Concordia and knew Ines, though wasn't in the same year as her. We made small talk and she asked how old I was and I said, "Twenty-six" again and everyone heard me. I was apparently going with the lying about my age thing, though wasn't sure to what extent or for how long or even for what purpose. It felt like I would eventually come up with an excuse in my head to rationalize this.

Mira seemed uninterested in me and quickly escaped our conversation. Just as Brent was about to get up to go grab another bottle of wine, we heard the front door being opened and a group of people letting themselves in. "Hello," said a voice. Brent went to look and had a brief conversation with someone and then returned accompanied by firemen. One of the men explained that a neighbour had alerted them to a fire. He saw the trash can fire and said, "Is that it?" and then asked us to put it out. Brent apologized, went to the kitchen, filled a container with water, poured it on the trash can, repeated the process a second time. As they were about to leave, Brent asked the firemen to hold on and then mentioned that this was his return party and that he wanted a photo of himself with sexy firemen in the background. The firemen looked normal and not sexy, but agreed to pose. Laura photographed Brent wearing a fireman's helmet and smiling, with five firemen posing awkwardly in the background. She tweeted the picture, adding the caption, "My boyfriend is seven years old."

Around ten, Cristian returned home with Kyle. Brent told everyone that he was ordering drugs and asked me if I wanted anything and I replied that I was okay. He went to his room and made calls. Kyle complained that Cristian was thirty minutes late to meet him and seemed annoyed. "I thought you would be the same amount of late I was," Cristian said. Brent received a text message from someone instructing him to meet him at an address supposedly nearby. He ran out of the door and then returned twenty minutes later in a sweat and panting. People thanked Brent as he distributed the different orders. While handling his order, Cristian accidentally dropped the tiny plastic bag on himself. He laughed while licking his own pants, trying to retrieve the substance.

We locked the front door and left the house and headed to a bar. On the way there, I thought, "Do I want to get destroyed tonight?" a few times, but then couldn't think anything that had the shape of an answer. "You're fired," I imagined myself yelling at whatever brain module was responsible for my decision-making. I knew I would have to show up at work in less than twelve hours to finish a presentation, but couldn't get myself to head home. We walked in the venue, which looked about a quarter full, with most people forming a kind of huddle around the bar. A girl wearing a plastic tiara looked bored while DJing. I took out money from a sketchy looking ATM and then asked Cristian if he was getting anything.

"Yeah," said Cristian. "No, wait, hold on."

Cristian searched his pockets and then made a face.

"I had a ten dollars left," said Cristian. "I think I lost it. How did I lose it?"

"I'll buy you a beer," I said. "It's two for something, I think."

"Are you sure?" said Cristian. "Thank you. I don't know if I should have gotten drugs. I need to start budgeting again."

"When were you budgeting?" I said.

"Last year, when I moved out of my mom's house," said Cristian. "I remember, I was really motivated. I wanted to plan a budget, stick to it, pile up cash and then travel. I did it once. It worked that one time."

"You're never going anywhere," said Brent. "You can't save money. That's your main problem. You'll fuck up at some point, or you'll get fired, or something will happen to you that will make you go back to zero, or below zero. You need a job that pays you to fuck up. Fucking up is your best skill."

"It's true," said Cristian. He laughed. "I should put that on my resumé."

"That call centre place would give you a really good recommendation letter for that," said Brent. "I highly recommend this person for fucking up. He will not show up on time for any of his shifts. He will sleep with his coworkers and pretend it didn't happen. He will have an excellent attitude as he causes unnecessary mayhem and destruction."

"If they hire me with that resumé, it's my dream job," said Cristian.

We drank more beers. I went back to the sketchy ATM and saw Laura from afar, bored-dancing with Jeremy and Mira. I withdrew more money and then bought shots at the bar.

"This is kind of stupid," said Brent.

"We should tell her to put on better party music," said Cristian.

" 'Disco Star Wars,' " I said.

"We need to do something that would annoy Laura," said Brent.

"Like what?" said Cristian.

"Like we're those people that are partying too hard and we don't understand that everyone else is having a shit time," said Brent. "We need to be those people."

"Go dance on that table," said Cristian. "Do sexy dance moves. To 'Disco Star Wars.'"

"That would look insane," said Brent. "There's, like, six people dancing. I should do it in my underwear."

"You would get kicked out so fast," said Cristian.

"They wouldn't care if I took off my pants," said Brent. "It's a million degrees in here. There's us and twenty people and the staff. They would think it's funny."

"Would they?" said Cristian.

"Let's get in our underwear and go dancing with Laura," said Brent. "That would really piss her off. Come on, it'll be funny. Tiara girl will think it's funny. Look how bored she is."

"We can't do that," said Cristian, smiling.

"We just need to both be doing this and it'll be fine," said Brent. "The staff will think it's a thing. You're doing this with me."

"You're not going to pretend you're doing it and then back out at the last minute so that I look crazy without my pants on in the bar, right?" said Cristian.

"I won't," said Brent. "I am doing it. Come on."

"Okay," said Christian. "Hold on."

Cristian chugged a third of his beer. They began taking off their shoes and socks and looked at each other very seriously while doing so, as if afraid the other was going to back out. They both laughed. Cristian took off his belt and then pants, revealing boxers that had poker chips on them. Brent, wearing red briefs with a black waistband, ran across the room and began joke-dancing next to Laura, using her as a vertical pole. She laughed. Cristian danced casually next to Brent. Tiara girl laughed. Other people in the bar laughed. A few minutes later, Kyle also got in his underwear and began dancing. Then Jeremy and then Laura. Then I joined. Brent gave me a high-five for joining and seemed surprised that I had. I seemed surprised that I had. The dynamic in the bar was now completely different. People were excited, smiling, dancing, talking faster, louder. Getting drunk seemed purposeful again. I withdrew more money from the ATM and then alternated between drinking and dancing until closing time.

Around three, I put clothes back on and so did everyone else except Cristian and Brent, who were sharing a cigarette outside. Some of Laura's friends said goodbye and went home. Mira mentioned something about a bonfire and we decided to walk there. Everyone seemed a little drunk and better for it. Still in his underwear, Brent borrowed Kyle's skateboard and glided down the street, but then almost tripped and fell. A few streets later, we found the bonfire at a quiet location behind abandoned buildings.

Cristian sat close to the fire. I gave two dollars to someone in exchange for one of his beers, sat next to Cristian.

"You should put your pants back on now," Laura said to Christian. "Brent is putting on his. It's getting colder."

"No, I am okay," said Cristian. "I'll just sober up here for a while."

"I haven't been to an actual bonfire in a while," I said. "Hopefully I still know how to bonfire."

"We should burn something," said Cristian.

I looked around and noticed old copies of *The Mirror* in a pile nearby. I reached for a newspaper and handed it to Cristian. He began flipping through it.

"I got in late at work again this morning," said Cristian. "I think they're going to fire me, I don't know."

"Are you sure?" I said.

"It feels like it, the way they talk to me now," said Cristian. "It's okay, I'll just go get fired somewhere else."

He laughed. I liked how Cristian made fun of his failures in a detached manner, as if shit-talking someone who wasn't present. He seemed both obvious and oblivious to himself. In the newspaper's cinema section, Cristian found a long article previewing upcoming movies. He ripped out a page and crumpled the piece of paper into a ball and said, "I hate Julia Roberts," and then threw the ball into the fire.

"Why do you hate Julia Roberts?" I said.

"Do you know *Pretty Woman*, do you know that movie?" said Cristian. "It's this cheesy movie from the 90s. That was my dad's favourite movie when I was a kid. Julia Roberts plays a prostitute in it. My dad would drink beers and watch it every couple of weeks. That lasted something like eight years. I think he liked the idea of being rich and paying a movie star to have sex with him. My mom didn't care, so that didn't seem strange to me. It was just his movie. One time, I was older, I remember watching it with him, and there's a scene where Julia Roberts gives the guy a plastic wrapper, and I remember thinking, 'What's this? What's inside the wrapper? Candy? Why would she give candy to him now? That's odd.' Then I realized that she was handing him a condom and that they were going to have sex, or maybe their shadows would be having sex. Then I felt something, and I am pretty sure that was my first boner."

"That's funny," I said. "How do you remember that?"

"I don't know, but that's why I hate Julia Roberts," said Cristian. "If I see her face somewhere, I automatically think about that."

"Do you think you would have a boner if you watched that scene today?" I said. "The condom scene."

"Maybe," said Cristian. "You mean a nostalgia boner?"

"Or like a memory boner," I said. "Your body remembering the boner."

"I don't know," said Cristian. He laughed. "Maybe."

"Cristian, you should really put your pants back on now," said Laura.

"I am fine," said Cristian.

"It's not funny anymore," said Brent. "It's even weird a little now."

"I'll put them on soon," said Cristian. "I am fine for now."

Brent and Cristian argued back and forth for about five minutes about the necessity of Cristian putting his pants back on. After

Cristian caved in, Jeremy said that he had leftover beers in his fridge and that we should go get them. We decided to leave the bonfire. I noticed that Brent's energy level had decreased and that he was starting to look tired and ready to pass out. A few streets later, Jeremy stopped in front of an apartment building and said, "Won't be long." While waiting for him, Brent took out a small plastic bag from his back pocket. I grabbed my phone and photographed Brent looking uninterested and groggy while ingesting drugs and saved the image as a wallpaper. Jeremy came back out, seemed excited, shouted, "Success!"

We walked to Mont Royal and sat near the mountain. I had spaced about a million beers, felt mediumly drunk, didn't feel tired. I thought about having to be at work in a few hours and then imagined myself showing up there without having slept. The imaginary situation felt good. I thought about things like self-esteem, success, relationships and self-improvement all being for other people. I thought about self-sabotage being for me.

Later, I stared at what looked like the beginning of a sunrise.

By setting the alarm on my phone for ten, I knew I would get to work late enough for people to notice but not late enough for them to complain. I had slept less than three hours, had a body that felt like a bag of oatmeal, didn't want to exit the bed. I wanted my pillow to be a supercomputer, allowing me to complete work tasks by rolling my head around on it.

I got up, didn't change clothes, drank water, grabbed my bike, left the house. I biked downhill half-awake. Daylight seemed impossible to ignore. Pollen attacked my face. I saw bikes flowing between vehicles like liquid, anxious people alone in their little cars, honking. Any minor bump in the road felt like it had the potential to kill me. Fifteen minutes later, I locked my bike to a small tree. I thought, "My hangover is the only thing keeping me alive."

I tried making a discreet entrance, but then Julian saw me and noticed my lateness and made a face. On the way to my computer, I passed by a person playing a knight game. The person whacked a dragon with a broadsword and looked bored. I sat at my desk and began doing things to my computer to the rhythm of other people doing things to their computers. I checked my work emails and then clicked on the calendar tab and saw that I had no meeting scheduled for the day, which was unusual. People at the studio seemed to share some sort of obsessive-compulsive meeting disorder. Above all, they liked to create meetings, give them names, express themselves through their meeting-creation skills, critique and backtalk other people's meetings.

My main task for the day was to finish putting together a Power-Point that I would be presenting the next day. The studio was owned by a parent company, which was based in Los Angeles. Because of its aggressive sales strategies and profit-oriented approach, the parent company was frequently shit-talked by people on the internet, some of whom were even technically employed by it. Sometimes, executives from California flew in, visited us, complained and then left. While they complained, we took notes. The executives were mostly marketing bros in their thirties or forties. They liked basketball, money, workout routines, didn't care about art or personal expression or advancing the medium. Most of them looked like they would be climbing the corporate ladder until they ran out of oxygen. We usually received ambiguous or contradictory directives from them, probably because they themselves had received ambiguous or contradictory directives from their superiors. Every year, many games were green-lighted for production, only to be cancelled later.

Trying to work, I couldn't concentrate or get any of the slides to look or feel satisfying. I wanted to write, "P.S. I am sleep-deprived," as a disclaimer on every slide. From afar, I saw Julian giving a tour of the studio to an executive wearing a blazer, a black tie and rimless glasses. They stopped near my desk and chatted for a full minute before addressing me.

"Michael, I'd like to introduce you to Thomas, our game designer on Next-Generation Scrabble," said Julian, turning to me. "Thomas, this is Michael Fahey. He's the senior executive producer on Scrabble and a number of other projects in Los Angeles."

"Nice to meet you," I said, shaking Michael Fahey's hand.

"Thomas is working on a PowerPoint presentation for you guys," said Julian. "It'll be awesome. Right, Thomas?"

"Absolutely," I said. "Very awesome PowerPoint presentation. Cutting-edge graphics."

"Make sure you put 3D explosions and T. Rexes in there," said Michael Fahey, smiling. "Make it awesome!"

Julian laughed politely at Michael Fahey's joke. I didn't feel like laughing, but forced myself to, to appear normal.

I felt like my face was going to crack open.

After they left, I checked my phone and saw that I had a new voicemail. I got up and went to a small room and listened to the recorded message. Someone from my bank wanted to talk to me because my account had been flagged for suspicious activity. I hated talking on the phone, didn't want to call back. "Can't I just text them?" I thought. When I called back, the bank employee asked me questions about recent transactions on my account. I explained that those transactions were all made by me, including consecutive withdrawals from the sketchy ATM. Validating the transactions with the person from the bank got me to relive most of the previous night, which made me feel good. I felt positive about my bank and from now on wanted my bank to call me every time I was hungover.

"Last night was like five nights in one," I typed later in a short email to Shannon. I decided that this was all the email would say. On Facebook, I saw that Laura had posted photos from the night before. In one of the photos, I looked like I was about to explode. I received a message from Julian telling me the presentation might take place late today instead of tomorrow and asking if I was ready. I replied I was. I wasn't. I felt severely tired, wanted to squeeze my face between the letters J and K on my keyboard. I somehow managed to power through and put together something passable. A little after four, I went to the bathroom and applied hair product. I looked only marginally better. I hadn't bothered shaving or wearing clothes that would make me look like a young professional who takes himself seriously.

About half an hour later, I sat at a table in the conference room and waited for my turn to talk. I should have been nervous, but was too exhausted to produce the proper amount of anxiety. The executives were in a good mood, joking, seemed eager to go out for drinks later. I felt brain dead and maybe clinically dead. I pretended to take notes in my notebook. I always carried a notebook to meetings to pretend taking notes.

After being introduced by Julian, I pulled up the PowerPoint presentation on the projector and stood in front of a roomful of theoretically important executives and managers from the studio.

"Hi all," I said to complete silence. "So, Scrabble."

"Next-Generation Scrabble," said Julian, correcting me.

"Right," I said. "Next-Generation Scrabble. I prepared this presenation to get you all up to date with what we're doing. This is the first slide. Wait, hold on."

I moved to reach the keyboard and then pressed a key to dismiss the opening slide and introduce the second. I felt like I was going in slow motion, couldn't focus. I wasn't sure I remembered what the second slide contained. I stared at the new slide for a few seconds, which featured a screenshot, three bullet points and the question, "What is Next-Generation Scrabble?" I became aware that everyone in the room was waiting for me to resume talking.

"So it's pretty simple," I said. "We're basically adapting the version we did for lower-end phones last year, and taking advantage of the iPhone's advantages. I mean, capabilities. Taking full advantage of the iPhone's capabilities."

"What about playing online with your friends?" said one of the executives.

"No," I said. "I mean, we'll get to that. Sorry."

"Are you drunk?" said Julian in a mocking tone. Most people around the table laughed. He was smiling, trying to lighten up the room.

"Oh, I am not drunk now," I said. "I was nine hours ago." Everyone in the room thought I was joking and laughed again.

I felt awkward.

I continued going through the slides, each one feeling like a minor victory. My presentation was boring and fact oriented except for the final slide, which was a joke slide I had put in there for no reason other than to entertain myself. The slide's header read, "To sum up, our goal:" and was accompanied by a pie chart with the word "Profit" written on all four slices. Looking at it on the projector, I wasn't sure why I had decided to include this. After a few seconds of silence, Julian made a face, didn't seem like he approved of the joke slide, but then Michael Fahey said, "Yes!" and, "This is my dream pie chart," while smiling and pointing at the screen.

Everyone else in the room laughed and clapped a little and went along with it.

I wanted to stalk Romy's Facebook, but then typing her name in the little box failed to bring up her profile. I realized that she had deactivated her account. For a second, I felt bad, as if all my stalking was what had made her quit Facebook.

"The Rave Cave," read a sign someone had put up above the basement door in the backyard. "That's what I am naming it, the basement underneath the house," said Brent later, explaining the sign.

I didn't have a strong sense of accomplishment with video games. Most of the titles I had worked on were no longer available, had become technologically obsolete. Searching for them on Google only brought up broken domain names or outdated JPEGs. The internet didn't seem to remember them. I wasn't sure I remembered them either.

At night, I was either going to parties or hiding in my room. I felt as if my goal overall was to be invited to all the parties, but never go. I was starting to view parties as an infinitely renewable resource, like I could skip one and all that would do is make ten more appear. Still, it was comforting to know that parties were there if I needed them to be there, like a low-hanging fruit.

Caring enough to put on hair products for class, not caring enough to put them on for work.

"I am still okay with having sex with someone because we're both sexy," said Shannon. It was a few minutes after our final class of the semester and we were having beers at a pub near Concordia. Neither of us would be taking classes over the summer and were prepared to see each other less often. "But I feel like my standards for who I want to sleep with are getting really obscure."

"That's just consumption," I said, "like if you buy shampoo every week for a year, you'll start noticing things about the shampoos that you wouldn't have noticed before, and you might feel attracted to weird shampoos, like a berry-avocado shampoo, and you'll start wishing you could combine some of the qualities of the shampoos, and then you'll develop this fantasy in your head of a perfect shampoo that doesn't actually exist."

"That sounds like what I am saying," said Shannon. "I just wish Brian would move here. He's my perfect shampoo."

"Why doesn't he?" I said.

"I don't want to talk about it," said Shannon. "Is anything going on in your romantic life? Probably not."

"Not really," I said. "I try to hit on girls sometimes, but then I am so cynical about it that I usually give up pretty fast. It's like I don't expect it to go anywhere, but still find it entertaining, so why not. It's sad."

"You should hit on Romy," said Shannon.

"I don't even know if she exists," I said. "Like I still haven't physically met her. She could be just a girl who lives inside my computer that I email with from time to time."

"Or a lonely trucker," said Shannon.

"And I would be okay with that, like, I would get where the trucker is coming from," I said.

"Romy exists, you'll run into her soon," said Shannon.

"If we're only emailing and never meet, it's kind of nice to be able to think, 'I can't fuck this is up,' though," I said.

"Maybe they forgot," said Cristian. He still hadn't been fired and seemed vaguely annoyed by that.

I felt like half a sexual being, like I could either take my sexuality or leave it.

Walking through the food court on my way to work, it suddenly dawned on me that it was all cyclical. We were paid to gather in an office and produce software that extracted money from consumers. Sprinkled around our office were food court restaurants and other stores whose business model relied heavily on our conscious and repeated decision to never bring lunch. It wasn't too difficult to imagine the food court's employees going home at night, feeling exhausted after a long and probably infuriating day at work, maybe playing a video game on their phones as a way to relax, think nothing, inadvertently spending money on titles by companies like ours. Maybe there was nothing being accomplished in this building, just money being passed around, man-hours being lost.

In the middle of an aisle at Chapters, I began reading an interview with William Faulkner from a book of interviews with writers. The Chapters inside the mall had become one of my favourite places to escape from work during my lunch break. In the interview, William Faulkner said something about a person's only responsibility being to his or her artistic work, and that the person should be completely amoral and borrow or steal from anybody and everybody if stealing meant completing the work. I reached for my phone and photographed the passage.

I sat on the couch in the common area while Brent borrowed a chair from the kitchen table. It was late April and we had planned a meeting to discuss year two of Cinedrome, but Cristian was late. Eventually, he opened the front door and brought in a bike, which was odd because he didn't own a bike. The bike was bright yellow and had a large sticker on the frame that said "Valley." Brent asked where the bike was from and Cristian explained that someone near his mom's house had set up an effigy on their front lawn for a teenager who had passed away after being hit by a car. Next to the effigy was the kid's bike.

"You stole a dead kid's bike?" said Brent.

"Yeah, but it's not like I am hurting anyone," said Cristian. "I really needed one. I am late for work all the time."

"It's a dead kid's bike," said Brent. "There's some bad karma on that shit."

"They left it right there, on the lawn," said Cristian. "Someone else would have taken it if I hadn't seen it first. Maybe they didn't want to look at it anymore and just wanted someone to get rid of it for them. You don't know that."

"Okay, just, forget it," said Brent. "Listen."

Brent took control of the meeting. He went over the basics and explained that we would be using the same formula as the previous year. Cinedrome would be presenting one movie every Friday from nine to eleven p.m., promote its events over Facebook only, charge nothing at the door, distribute popcorn in the audience for free, sell beer illegally for profit, ask for donations after the movie. We discussed different solutions to avoid getting noise complaints from neighbours or being fined for selling beer without a permit. The goal of the cinema wasn't to make money, just to be sustainable. We had no budget but very little costs, since Brent owned the projector and we owned the chairs and screen.

"If we make money, we could pay back the electricity bill," said Cristian. "I don't think anyone really wants to pay that."

"If we can," said Brent. "It depends on how much we make. I might want to get a new camera if we make a lot of cash over the summer. Don't worry about the electricity bill, though. They would never dare cut us off. They wouldn't do that."

It felt like I was trying to use social networks as a way to prototype myself. If I posted something online that was witty or depressing in a funny way, I received positive reinforcement. If I posted something that wasn't fully thought out or only made sense to me, I received no reinforcement, which was negative reinforcement. I wanted to fine-tune myself, reject all parts of myself that didn't produce positive feedback.

According to a video game blog, "play" was defined as "free movement within a more rigid structure."

"This is my cocaine shirt," said Brent. He was wearing sunglasses and a yellow Hawaiian shirt with pirate swords and flags on it. "I can only wear this shirt if I am doing cocaine."

"What are you doing tonight?" I asked.

"Cocaine," said Brent. "Bye."

Montreal had pretty girls to a point where some of them seemed to forget they were pretty and just thought of themselves as normal.

"I think Ines is slowly moving out," I typed to Shannon on Facebook Chat. "Her boyfriend just got this new apartment and he lives alone, so she's been mostly staying there and using her room here as a studio lately. She still pays rent, though."

"So your house is all boys now," typed Shannon. "Is it strange without her?"

"Brent's girlfriend is here a lot, though," I typed. "It's not weird without Ines, but the power dynamic is different. We all have additional roles, like if Christian brings a girl home, Brent's the one who's nice to her the next day now. I think he's trying to be the responsible one."

"I thought you were the responsible one," typed Shannon.

"I am the not-even-going-to-try one," I typed.

About thirty minutes before attendees were supposed to start showing up, Cristian and I did a cleaning blitz of the kitchen and bathroom and common area. I thought about the true purpose of hosting Cinedrome in the backyard, which was maybe to trick ourselves into panic cleaning the house once a week. It was the second Friday of May and the first Cinedrome of the year. The weather was cooperating. Cristian set out chairs, arranging them in multiple rows facing the screen. Our chairs came in different models and sizes and quality, from less broken to mostly broken. Some were stools.

As people began walking in, Brent lit dollar store candles and placed them near the front door and around the backyard. "Rave Cave," someone said, reading the sign above the basement door aloud. Within forty minutes, most of our chairs had found guests willing to sit on them. Before starting the projection, Brent improvised a brief speech about Cinedrome, thanking everyone for coming and then introducing *The Holy Mountain*. I sat through the first third of the film, which had dreamlike visuals and a nonsensical plot. Cristian kept grinning and nodding while staring at the screen, seemed amazed and awestruck. A few attendees in the back unsubtly smoked weed. "At least it's a good movie for them to do that," said Brent in a quiet voice. "There's always some asshole smoking weed in the back. It doesn't even matter what movie we're showing. It could be *Schindler's List* and someone would get really stoned and start laughing at Ralph Fiennes' face or something."

We sold cheap beer and ran out and I had to sprint to the convenience store to purchase more on at least two separate occasions. I could take beers from our stash and drink them if I wanted to, but then I wasn't sure if they would end up making me feel slow and headache-y the next day. I wanted the beers' packaging to specify what kind of hangover I was going to get from drinking them.

After the screening, I collected donations at the door, mostly loose change with some paper bills mixed in, then cleaned the backyard by picking up discarded beer cans and bottles. By the time I was done, most people had left or were about to leave, though a few were still hanging around the house, purchasing our leftover beers, texting, desperately seeking something to do as if soul-searching for a reason to live. Entering the kitchen, I saw that Cristian was leaning against the fridge and talking to someone about mystery novels. The girl had a small body frame, looked about twenty, had messy, shoulder-length black hair and was wearing simple clothes and worn-out shoes.

"Do you know that people used to write to Arthur Conan Doyle because they thought Sherlock Holmes was a real person and they wanted him to solve mysterious crimes or murders?" said Cristian.

"I didn't know that," said the girl. "I haven't read any of the books, but my dad was once in a play where he was Arthur Conan Doyle being haunted by the ghost of Sherlock Holmes. All I remember from it is that he was wearing a cloth over his head as a shawl and said, 'I shall laugh while I watch him roast' in a deep voice."

"I wish people would write to me to solve their murders," said Cristian.

"I want a Sherlock Holmes where he gets up at six p.m. and does nothing for five hours and then pre-drinks in an alley before trying to pick up girls in sketchy bars," I said.

"I could write that," said Cristian.

"Do we have more beer?" I said.

"There's two left," said Cristian. "You can have them if you want. Look in the back."

"Is that okay?" I said.

"Yeah, sure," said Cristian. "Take them."

"I like the jellyfish," said the girl.

"Ines made those," I said. "What's your name?"

"Romy," said the girl.

"I am Thomas," I said. "Nice to meet you. I live here also, Cristian's my roommate."

"How long have you been doing this?" said Romy.

"This is the second year, but I wasn't here last year," I said. "I only moved here in the winter."

"Are you all film majors?" said Romy.

"I just like movies," said Cristian. "I get really absorbed in them."

"Brent's a filmmaker," I said. "He makes music videos and stuff."

"Wedding videos," said Cristian.

"Cinedrome is mostly his thing," I said. "I am not that interested in movies. I am not even sure I am interested in people."

"Why do you say that?" said Romy.

"I am just kidding," I said.

"I'll be back," said Cristian, walking away to go talk to Brent.

"It's nice," said Romy. "I have this stupid zine that I don't want to do anymore. I just want to get rid of the last copies. Maybe I could sell them here."

"Wait," I said. "So you have a zine?"

"Yeah," said Romy.

I said wait a second time and then asked if her last name was Nelson. She said it was. I explained that we knew each other and had exchanged emails a few times. I hadn't recognized her because the pictures of her on Facebook were all blurry or dated. I presumed that she hadn't recognized me because she hadn't made the effort of stalking me.

"There were a bunch of times where I thought we would meet but then we didn't," I said. "Shannon would be like, 'Did you see Romy?' and then she would look around and it was always, 'I guess she's gone, oh well.' I wasn't sure you actually existed."

"No, I exist," said Romy.

"That's good," I said. "What were you doing before this?"

"I was supposed to meet this guy at the mountain this afternoon," said Romy, "and I thought I knew where he was, but then I decided to take a shortcut and I got lost. I ended up having to slide down a steep slope to get back on the main path, and while I was sliding down trying not to die, I saw someone else that I know. She just happened to be passing by. She said hi and I said, 'Hi, what's up?' trying to pretend that I didn't look completely stupid doing what I was doing."

Romy laughed a nervous laugh.

"So how did you end up here?" I said. "You don't have Facebook anymore."

"I got it back two days ago," said Romy. "I just compromised with myself by deleting people I didn't want to think about anymore. Shannon texted me about this. She said she was coming, but I don't think she showed up."

"You can only half-rely on her," I said. "She thinks different things every six hours. Sometimes she gets really depressed and can't get out of bed. Have you ever been out with her, though?"

"Only a few times," said Romy. "We're not close or anything, I usually just run into her when I go out. One time, I went to her apartment and she was writing a letter to this guy from San Francisco. I don't know if she told you about him."

"Brian Something," I said.

"Him," said Romy. "I didn't know what was going on. It looked like some serious stalker shit."

"She writes him long letters and he probably just reads half of them," I said, "and then it makes her sad because the letter was so beautiful in her head that she thought it would change things and make him want to move here. She has no emotional, like, immunity system. She means well, she's just spontaneous and constantly having emotions and never has any distance from anything."

"I know," said Romy. "I don't hate it."

I laughed a little, began to feel a premature sense of kinship with Romy. She seemed uncomplicated and not stressed with things, the kind of person that could spell "elephant" with a W and know it's wrong and not care. Cristian rejoined our conversation and informed us that Brent and Laura were going to a launch party for a magazine run by McGill students. I asked him what he was doing and he said, "Nothing," and then explained that he felt inspired by *The Holy Mountain* and wanted to stay in and note down ideas before forgetting them. I said, "Okay." I wasn't sure if he was being serious or not.

Ten minutes later, Romy, Brent, Laura and I left the house. I walked beside Romy and felt myself wanting to impress her a little. I started worrying about my hair or face or what I was wearing or posture or the position of my hands. I didn't do terrible at talking to her, but didn't do excellent either. I thought, "I suck, my personality sucks, I wish I could photoshop my personality."

We entered a building, ascended the stairs to the third floor, saw that the space where the launch was taking place was an art gallery. At the door, names of DJs appeared on a large poster that was duct-taped to a wall. "It could have just said, 'Loud techno music,'" said Brent. Romy didn't have money on her, so I paid for the both of us. To stamp us in, a tall girl with a black marker wrote "Babe" on the back of my right hand and then on the back of Romy's hand. Inside, people were either dancing in the front or standing in the back, socializing in little teams of five or six.

"Sorry you had to pay for me," said Romy.

"That's okay," I said. "I am used to it. Everyone's broke."

"Montreal," said Romy. "Everyone's broke, everyone's partying anyway. I only moved here for school, so this is still funny to me."

"Where are you from originally?" I said.

"Just, Ontario," said Romy. "My dad was born in Texas, but he's been living here for a while. He still has a strong Southern accent and gets looks in public when he orders at restaurants. I am going back there soon, for the summer. I'll be here again in the fall, to finish my last two classes and graduate. I honestly don't know how I'll survive being home, but I don't speak French, so it's hard to get a job here."

"It's kind of insane how you can function entirely in English here and not have to worry about French all that much," I said. "I mean, outside of getting a job. I have barely been using my French since moving into the Cinedrome house."

"Are you from Montreal?" said Romy.

"No," I said. "I lived in Quebec City before moving here. It's much harder to get by if you don't know French there. There was this guy I worked with, he had moved there from Halifax, and all he knew were basic greetings and the French word for chicken. He would go in restaurants and say 'Poulet?' until someone brought him warm food."

"That guy could be my French tutor," said Romy. "Do you think they sell beer here? Wait, I still don't have money."

"I still have the two from Cinedrome," I said. "Hold on."

I reached for my backpack and unzipped it and then looked for the aluminum cans. I handed her one.

"Thank you," said Romy.

"You should see Cristian sneaking in beer everywhere," I said. "He's really good at it. He has all these strategies, like, if it doesn't work the first time, he'll go in an alley and drink beers there alone and try again later. He has kind of a drinking habit, but it's not an expensive one. It's more like a time-consuming one."

"Why didn't he come out with us?" said Romy.

"I have no idea. Cristian goes out a lot," I said. "Nightlife is pretty much just life for him. He works, like, twenty hours per week, so if he's not partying, he's either working or sleeping all day to recuperate. I don't know why he stayed home tonight."

"Maybe he's putting up a Craigslist ad about solving people's murders for them," said Romy. "I could murder you and ask him to solve it."

"That would make him happy," I said.

"I find it impossible to get anything done in Montreal sometimes," said Romy. "I want to concentrate and be productive, but then there's a distraction and all of a sudden I am at a party and it's three days later and I still haven't accomplished anything."

"I think some people secretly don't want you to be productive, because if you are, it puts more pressure on them to accomplish something," I said. "They want you to go out with them all the time so that everyone's mediocre and no one has to try."

Romy laughed.

"You really think that's what they're trying to do?" said Romy.

"Maybe more subconsciously than consciously," I said. "A lot of people go into art programs and then realize that it won't go anywhere for them and quit, so they feel bitter about it a little."

"I see what you mean," said Romy.

"The only way to survive is to feel awkward at parties and leave," I said. "Otherwise, if you like people and feel comfortable around people and don't get bored of people, I could see partying being a full-time job."

"I've done that, though," said Romy. "Just, like, leave."

"That's good," I said. "Feeling defeated by the party. We're pioneering a new form of partying."

"Lonely partying," said Romy.

"Exactly," I said. "We should get a patent for that."

Romy finished her beer. I was still halfway through mine and tried catching up, but then the music stopped abruptly and lights were turned back on. "What's going on?" a person near us said. Two police officers appeared at the door. Someone yelled that police cars were outside and that they were shutting down the venue. One of the DJs shouted a few times that they should keep going and pay whatever fine they get, but he was mostly ignored. More officers appeared. Most people stood there awkwardly. I stood there awkwardly. An officer interrogated the tall girl at the door. The rest were being surprisingly hands-off, not pressuring anyone to do anything, just waiting, arms crossed, as if assuming people would get bored, clean up after themselves, leave. All they seemed to be wanting was for the crowd to exit the building. Finally, the tall girl at the door got up on a chair and yelled, "Everyone, get the fuck out," which got people to move.

Outside, people were loitering, stalling, trying to make new plans.

"There has to be something else going on," said Brent. "A house party, something."

"I don't know of anything else," said Laura. "Why don't we just go back to your house and have a house party there?"

"We could do that," said Brent.

"I mean, no one here knows what they're doing," said Laura. "They could all come."

"Yeah, you're right," said Brent. "I don't want to go to some bar. Fuck it. Let's do that."

"You would be okay with that, right, Thomas?" said Laura.

I said, "Sure, yeah," but then saw that Brent was already going around and yelling, "House party at 4562 St-Dominique." While I waited with Romy, Laura talked to people she knew and tried to convince them to come. A light rain began to fall. A few minutes later, Brent said, "Let's just go." We walked back home followed by a group of about thirty. Back at the house, I opened the front door and found Cristian sitting on the couch in the common area, looking focused and writing something on a piece of paper.

"They got shut down, I think we're having a house party," said Brent. "I hope that's okay."

"I was just working on a business proposal," said Cristian. "It's fine though, I am almost done."

"Cool," said Brent. He made a face, looked like he wasn't sure what Cristian meant by "business proposal," but didn't feel like asking.

Brent brought out computer speakers from his room and put on rap music. He texted someone from the magazine launch, tried to convince the person to bring leftover alcohol from the party by telling him he could sell it here. The person texted back, "Maybe" and then later, "No." There was no alcohol in the house, meaning what people had brought with them was all they had. I checked my phone for the time and saw that it was almost two a.m. Brent, Laura and I pooled our money together and gave Cristian twenty-nine dollars, convincing him to head to the convenience store and purchase whatever alcohol he could get. Stores were prohibited by law from selling alcohol after eleven, but Cristian had special tricks and was good at getting bored night clerks to sell beer to him anyway. After Cristian left, I retreated to my room with Romy while the house party went on in other rooms. We sat side by side on my bed, with empty space between us.

"Do you mind if I ask," said Romy. "Shannon was talking about you the other day. She didn't know how old you were. It was like this big secret. 'How old is he?' No one knew."

"Twenty-six," I said.

I was getting used to hearing myself lie about my age, to a point where the lie didn't feel like a lie anymore. It was like the lie had mutated, become some sort of split truth, one that said I had two ages, a public age of twenty-six and a private age of twenty-seven.

"That's not so bad," said Romy. "I don't know what I was expecting, though. You could have said any number."

"Fifty-nine," I said. "Retirement party next month."

"Exactly," said Romy. "I would have thought that makes sense. I would have thought any number made sense."

"I felt like an alien a lot in class," I said, "because of the age difference with some people, but also because English is my second language. And because some people seemed to come from classic literary backgrounds, like their parents were authors or they did a special creative writing program in high school or something. I don't come from a classic literary background at all. It's more like a I-hate-myself background."

Romy laughed a little.

"I had people like that in my classes," said Romy, "whose parents were authors. You can tell they're going to write books even if they have to buy them and read them themselves. Some people were just lost. They were doing creative writing because it was the best thing they could think of. It was just two, three years of therapy for them."

"What type were you?" I said.

"The second, I guess," said Romy.

She laughed nervously. From a distance, I heard Cristian's voice and then Brent's voice. I said, "Wait, hold on." I got up and walked to the common area. I saw that Cristian had returned with a box of Pabst Blue Ribbon and was doing a little dance, as if celebrating a touchdown. I thought, "Awesome guy trying to figure out life." Brent said, "How much was it?" and Cristian replied, "You owe me six dollars." Brent made a face and said, "Well, whatever, fuck it." Cristian, Laura, Brent and me each grabbed a can from the box and then Brent distributed the rest like candy to random people around the house. I went back to my room and sat next to Romy. She looked level-headed and not drunk. We shared the beer.

"I am supposed to graduate after the fall semester, but I don't know what I am doing after," said Romy. "I can't really apply to MFAs, like, I haven't been published anywhere or done anything. The only place that published me is this Tumblr that has pictures of cats inside things, like a cat sitting inside a mailbox. I sent them a picture of my cat. I don't think the MFAs would be impressed by that."

"They still look at your portfolio, though," I said.

"That's the problem," said Romy. "All my stories have characters that have no ambition and think dating in Montreal is the absolute worst. I don't know what I am trying to tell myself. Earlier this year, I was seeing this guy and we were in a polyamorous relationship and I didn't even know it. He hadn't told me. Is that normal to you? I didn't know the other girl, we were just both sleeping with him."

"So it wasn't a love triangle," I said. "It was more like two arrows pointing at the same thing."

"Yeah," said Romy. "Lev was really cool."

She smiled. I thought, "If she's interested in cool guys, I am fucked." I barely felt like a person, never mind a cool one. I thought, "Maybe all I have to do is make her think that I like myself and that I am a generic, bullshit cool person."

"Do you still see him?" I said.

"Lev's in New York now," said Romy. "He emails me from time to time. Sometimes I email him back."

I placed my left arm on the bed, touching her side. We were still sitting side by side, but there was no more space between us. I felt like she was letting me come closer. I didn't want to force anything on her, didn't want to be too aggressive but didn't want to be too subtle either. "Push forward, move forward, always forward," my penis whispered. It felt like everything I said or did was just a yes in disguise. I became aware that the house party was making less noise, meaning a lot of people had left or were about to leave. There was a brief silence followed by a longer silence. Then Romy stood up.

"I think I'll go," said Romy. She smiled. "Thank you for having me."

I said, "Thank you for coming," and smiled. Then I thought of different spellings of the word "Goddamn." We said goodbye and she left. I closed the door to my room and then drowned most of my thought channels in negative self-talk. I checked Facebook and HTMLGIANT and then maybe six other websites. Then I didn't know what to do anymore. I sat on my bed and stared at the ceiling for a few minutes. "Why would I have any advice for you?" said the ceiling. I wanted to dig a hole into myself, bury myself into myself, decompose. Though the house party was still vaguely going on, I felt like I was done socializing, had spent all my social points on Romy, would have to sit alone in the dark for a while and wait for the points to regenerate themselves before being able to interact with people again.

Then someone knocked on my door. I opened and saw Romy and made a face. "I completely forgot to check the time," said Romy. "It's so much more late than I thought it was." She laughed nervously. She explained that the metro was closed and that she didn't want to pay for a cab. "Do you want to sleep on the couch?" I said. "I think people will be leaving soon. We can just hang out until then." Romy mouthed, "Okay." I closed the door to my room and then turned around and saw that she was replying to a text message on her phone. We both sat on my bed and then I lay down. We made small talk. She lay on her side, with her back facing me and holding her phone close to her body. I changed position, wasn't sure where to place my hands. A full minute passed. Her phone vibrated again. She pressed the small plastic buttons to compose a response. We stopped saying things. The voices coming from the common area were becoming fainter. Her phone vibrated again, but this time she looked at the screen and then put it aside. We didn't move for another full minute. I focused on the sound of her inhaling and exhaling. It seemed compact, like a laser beam, as if travelling from her mouth directly to my ear. I thought, "What do I want?" and it seemed like what I wanted was to kiss her gently and then maybe less gently. Then I thought, "No, what do I really want?" and it felt like the answer to that was located on some sort of secret mental plane, one I didn't have access to.

Either she fell asleep or I passed out or both those things happened.

We slept in my bed, but not together.

Alone. I woke up and saw that Romy was gone and then deduced that she had snuck out while I was still asleep. I went to the kitchen, opened the fridge, stared at the fridge's contents, decided to make fried tofu and eggs. "Tofu," I thought. "A meat-like sponge," I thought. I did more or less nothing for seven hours, eating, drinking tea, showering, reading unmemorable internet content, essentially nothing. Later, stalking Romy's Facebook page, I saw that a message had been posted on her Wall by someone I didn't know. The person was named Catherine and the message said something about not getting a rape-check call from Romy the night before and asking if she was okay. Romy had already added a comment that said, "Rape-free!" I stared at the words and felt confused and made a face. I thought, "Rape-free."

I wasn't sure if Romy's comment was referring to me or not. I reviewed the night before in my head, trying to see things from Romy's perspective instead of mine. Though I hadn't thought about raping her at all, we were still more or less strangers, so she had probably felt uncomfortable sharing a bed with me. I thought, "Maybe it'll just turn into something we can joke about later."

I imagined myself telling her, "Remember that time I didn't rape you?" but then that sounded more devastating than funny.

Titles for poems I wanted to write:

— I THINK ABOUT THINGS EITHER WAY TOO MUCH OR NOT NEARLY ENOUGH

   — ALCOHOL MAKES ME LESS CONCERNED ABOUT MY HAIR

   — ALL MY RELATIONSHIPS ARE AMBIGUOUS RELATIONSHIPS

   — I AM SORRY YOU ARE A POEM, POEM

   — THE PLURAL OF "DESIRE" IS "DISTRESS"

   — DON'T MAKE ME RETWEET MYSELF

   — I DID LAUNDRY IN OCTOBER, IT'S NOW JANUARY

   — I TAKE ANYONE HAVING SEX WITH ANYONE AS A KIND OF REJECTION

"Put a hat on a dog," said one of our games. "Sort jewels," said another. Though they looked harmless, our titles were usually fairly clever at exploiting players, getting them to shell out additional cash for extra items or features, or shaming them into continuing to play. I was starting to feel as if I no longer agreed on a moral level with what I was being told to work on. Then again, since my name was buried in an optional sub-menu, meaning no one would know I had worked on this, maybe I didn't have to care. Maybe I just had to endure.

On Facebook, a status update from Romy informed me that she was back in her hometown and had qualms about it.

Though I didn't want to, I could hear Brent and Laura having sex in Brent's room. It was the third week of May. I tried ignoring the noise and going back to sleep, but couldn't. I imagined swallowing a cyanide pill specifically designed for when roommates are having sex. A few minutes later, they finished and began talking. Laura said, "Do you think we were too loud?" and Brent replied, "Maybe." He added that the house's walls were paper-thin and that he had once heard me do intimate things in my room. Then he made fun of me a little for that. "I never heard Cristian when he was in that room," he said. This was not something Brent had told me directly, so I didn't know how or when he had heard me. I usually masturbated the way I imagined a ninja would masturbate, in secret and making only sounds that had failed at being silences.

At a used bookstore, I bought and then later read with interest a book titled *A History of Celibacy*.

Cristian started seeing someone named Marianna, a girl with dark hair and a nose ring who looked permanently drunk. One of the pros of the relationship, for him, seemed to be her bed, which he often described as "really comfortable," while smiling. "You don't understand," said Cristian. "It's a game changer." He slept several nights in a row at Marianna's apartment in Marianna's comfortable bed, couldn't get himself to escape the bed in the morning, kept showing up late to work. Eventually, he failed to wake up before five p.m. and was fired over the phone. This didn't seem to faze him, as he felt confident in his ability to run out of money and delay finding a new job for as long as possible. Later, Marianna broke up with him, which also didn't seem to faze him.

A part of me hated life, but then another part of me loved Montreal.

Hungover at work. "Endurance," I thought.

"It's no problem," said Shannon, hugging me a little. "Thanks for asking me." It was the second week of June, though not a particularly hot day. Shannon was wearing a baseball tee and a jean jacket with the sleeves cut short. Brent was shooting a music video for a local boy-girl duo and had enlisted Cristian and Kyle as actors. My role was "assistant director," though I wasn't sure what that would involve. Most of the video would be shot at night, in a secluded area near the train tracks. Brent needed someone to help out with makeup and costumes and so I had asked Shannon.

"How's your life?" I said. "I haven't really seen you since class ended."

"I know," said Shannon. She undid her hair, then redid her hair and then undid it again. "I am okay. Last night, I had cramps, so I just watched episodes of *Law & Order*. It's more exciting than it sounds. I have been doing a detox week. Everyone's been partying extra hard lately and that's when I decide to stop."

"Overtime partying," I said.

"Sobriety is tough when no one wants to be sober with you," said Shannon. "I just had to take a break. Things got really complicated this month. I have been attracted to this girl but I don't think she's into it, and then that turned into me waking up in the bed of this boy that I have been interested in for, like, two years. We finally slept together, but I don't remember anything about it except that he's beautiful. He said it was a mistake. It's kind of romantic, but only if you think of romance as adversarial."

"People are impossible," I said. "I wish I could just drink something and feel loved, the same way I can drink tea and feel awake."

"Why do people have such bad taste in people?" said Shannon.

"I am tired of people," I said. "I feel like I should write a poem that's called, 'I am tired of people.'"

"My friend Ben said exactly that the other day," said Shannon. "He said that he was tired of people and that all he wanted was an exact copy of himself. Then he looked confused and said that was a contradiction."

"Hi," said Brent coming out of his room. He was carrying a plastic bag filled with small flashlights of different colours. Earlier in the day, Brent had asked Cristian to shoplift flashlights from the dollar store. Cristian had pilfered about twenty-five, spread across six different trips. Brent introduced himself to Shannon and conversed with her a little.

"You look like someone I know," said Brent.

"People tell me all the time that I look like people, but I look at people and I don't feel like I look like them," said Shannon.

We moved to the backyard, where Kyle and Cristian were trying on their outfits. "We have to wait for Alex," said Brent. "She said she might be late. She lent some of her gear last night and needs to get her stuff back." Brent presented us with a mini-storyboard and explained the concept for the video, which was inspired by a seventeenth-century painting. Kyle would be playing "the creepy man" while Cristian would be "the animal man." Cristian's costume involved all-black clothing and a horse mask, which was too small to fully cover his face. Brent said the visible skin clashed with the rest of the outfit. Shannon suggested painting both sides of Cristian's face in black and Brent agreed this was a good idea. Shannon left to go look for face paint and came back from the store a few minutes later with mascara, which was all she could find. "This is going to work, don't worry," said Shannon.

She began applying mascara on the left side of Cristian's face, who was laughing. "Hold still," she said. Someone knocked on the front door. "That's probably Alex," said Brent. I went to open it.

"Thomas," said Pierre. I made a face. He coughed. I allowed him to come in and we made small talk in French. Pierre explained that our lease was about to expire and that he had spoken to Ines about renewing it. I asked Cristian and Brent if they knew about this and Cristian said that Ines had texted him, but that he had forgot to inform us until now. Pierre sat on the couch in the common area, looked tired, coughed again, stared at Cristian's horse costume. He asked if we still organized screenings and I replied, "From time to time," in French and he didn't add any follow-up question. Hearing myself talk, I became aware that my French now sounded robotic and not as smooth or natural as before. We switched to English to include other people in the conversation. Cristian asked a serious question about the lease renewal while wearing the horse mask and face paint. We signed the documents.

A few minutes later, just as Pierre was about to leave, Alex arrived. We grabbed Brent's equipment and moved on foot to the filming location. At the tracks, we discussed the shoot and began filming. Brent used the storyboard very loosely, did one take for most shots, filmed without using a tripod, simplified shots that were too ambitious, improvised a lot. I carried a clipboard around and pointed flashlights in various directions. "Assistant director," I thought. "Rape-free," I thought. I imagined staging a mutiny, firing Brent, taking over.

In the morning, I found a bottle of dishwashing liquid and washed off mascara all over the bathroom sink. About thirty minutes later, at work, I swiped my keycard, opened the main door, walked through an obstacle course of desks and chairs. "Dynamic panning," someone said. "Reverse-engineering," someone else said. I was late again and my synapses felt weak and dry, like damaged hair. I sat at my desk and was approached by Carl, the producer in charge of Scrabble. Carl was in his late thirties and balding and wore either a blazer with a tie or a navy blue hoodie. That morning, he was wearing the hoodie.

Carl reminded me that we had a review meeting scheduled and asked me various questions about Scrabble. I replied as best as I could, but felt only half-capable of handling a full conversation. Though I was starting to perceive Scrabble as incredibly meaningless, I said positive things about the project to Carl, mostly because he didn't seem to perceive Scrabble as incredibly meaningless. About fifteen minutes later, I grabbed my notebook and walked to a meeting room and then sat at a table. In the room with me were Carl, a game tester, a lead programmer, a lead artist and Julian. Carl spent the first few minutes of the meeting trying to get the projector in the room to work, which was how most meetings began.

"Are Pokémons immortal?" said the lead artist, while we were waiting. "Think about it. They don't show them dying in the game and they don't experience time. If you get a kitten, at some point it'll become an adult cat, then an old cat, then it dies. But Pokémons don't evolve un less they're at a certain level, so, in theory, they could stay infants forever."

"Hold on," said Carl. "Oh, good. I got it. Okay, we're going to start. Hi, everyone."

Carl put up visual work on the projector that the lead artist and his team had produced. We were shown an overview and then went through the different screens one by one.

"I don't know about this screen," said Julian. "The Create Game one. The text is too small. It makes the options hard to read."

"You might be right," said Carl.

"We can't really make the font bigger," said the lead artist. "We could if we removed a game option."

"What if you just moved the player pictures to the top," said Julian, "and aligned them there? That way you could even increase the size of the icons for all the game options."

"Yeah, but that would ruin the around-the-table feel we were going for," I said.

Julian made a face.

"Well," said Julian, "maybe we don't need that."

"If we remove that, it might look strange," I said. "We would be going halfway with the feel we were trying to achieve."

"I think it would look fine if we moved the player pictures to the top," said Julian.

We went back and forth a little on whether or not Julian's change was necessary. He seemed to think it was while I didn't think it was. Carl sided with Julian by default. No one else in the room had an opinion. I tried to convince Carl and Julian by talking about the around-the-table feel and restating what our original intentions were, but they either didn't seem to follow or didn't feel like backing down.

After the meeting, back at my desk, I thought, "I don't care," and then, "But this is really dumb," and couldn't tell if I was angry or not. I made a face while staring at my computer monitor. I wanted to headbutt the screen, get up, storm out. I checked my email inbox and saw that I had received a new message that said, "Your Amazon order has shipped." The email seemed to have a calming effect on me. I thought about the William Faulkner quote that I had photographed with my phone, the one about your only obligation being towards your artistic work, even if completing the work meant being amoral. I decided that I didn't care anymore and that I was officially mentally checking out and that from now on, I was going to prioritize my personal work at all times and not bother with work tasks unless I absolutely had to. "Free movement within a rigid structure," I thought.

I put on music and opened Microsoft Word and began working on a poem.

"The best part about Montreal is that it's cheap compared to other cities," said Brent. He had just finished shooting additional scenes for the music video in the Rave Cave and was now talking loudly to someone on Skype. "The worst part is that there's no money. It's always this, 'Can you do me a favour?' bullshit and never, 'I have all this cash to burn, let's make something that's super expensive but really fucking cool.'"

I wanted to scroll down Facebook until I reached year zero and then fell off Facebook entirely.

If the Hollywood sign was located inside my head, it would say "DESPERATE" in giant letters instead of "HOLLYWOOD."

The first Friday of July, we screened *Zardoz*. Over the last few weeks, Brent had presented more serious films, which had shrunk attendance. *Zardoz* was a good comeback movie, drawing a crowd large enough to generate the type of amplified noise that big crowds make.

Before the film, I talked to Ines, who I hadn't seen in a month.

"I am pretty much living at Matthew's now," said Ines. "I am just keeping my room here as a safety net. I miss this place, though. We should figure something out so that I don't have to handle rent anymore. Actually, do you want to take care of it from now on? I could just give you my share and you handle the rest with Pierre."

"Sure," I said.

"Great," said Ines. "There's the electricity bill as well, but that's a little more complicated."

I nodded.

Later, I sat next to Cristian and watched him watch *Zardoz*. In the movie, Sean Connery wears a red diaper and experiences trippy montages. About halfway through the film, I felt uninterested and eager to do something else. I walked in the house, saw Romy waiting in line for the bathroom, made a face. I had been convinced I wouldn't be seeing her until the fall, and so being in the same room as her now felt like violating some sort of hidden law of physics. I went up to her and said hi softly and then we hugged a little. She was wearing a plaid shirt and a pale red skirt over dark-coloured tights. I asked if she was just in town for a few days and she said, "No, I am back." She explained that she had felt unhappy back home and had found a loophole to return to Montreal. The person occupying the bathroom came out and Romy went in.

While waiting for her, I heard Brent shouting my name. I turned around and saw that a female cop and a male cop had entered the house and were looking around and seemed confused. "Cop couple," I thought.

"Talk to them," said Brent. He hurried to the backyard to warn Cristian. Our system to avoid getting caught selling beer involved stashing the beer in a suitcase, which could be quickly locked and then tossed in the shed. Brent wanted me to be the one who talked to cops because he was convinced that francophone police officers were biased against anglophone residents.

"We've received several noise complaints from your neighbours," said the female cop in French. Both officers were wearing camo pants and leather gloves. The female cop's insignia seemed shinier than the male cop's insignia. I was asked for ID. I handed the female cop a card with a photo of me on it. In the photo, I looked particularly large-headed.

"It's not the first time we've had complaints," said the male cop. "What are you doing here exactly?"

"We're screening a movie in our backyard," I said in French. "It should be over in half an hour."

"So everyone that's here?" said the female cop.

"They'll all be leaving to go somewhere else," I said. "Half an hour."

"We need to have a look," said the male cop.

I said, "Sure," and then led them to the backyard. I stepped outside and saw Cristian and Brent standing near the beer table with no beer suitcase or beer evidence in sight. The male and female cop surveyed the crowd scrupulously. "We need you to lower the sound," said the male cop. "It's too loud." I translated for Brent, who said, "No problem." Trying to be discreet, he walked past the screen and then lowered the volume of the speakers by turning a knob. I suddenly felt more appreciative of the power of knobs. The police officers looked only marginally satisfied, but had no further objection.

"If you want to do this, please, rent a proper venue," said the female cop. "Have a good night."

Shortly after they left, Brent exhaled loudly. He turned the volume back up and we resumed selling beer. Almost immediately after the screening, we all moved to Casa Del Popolo, which was a short walk from the house. Brent, Cristian and I snuck in leftover beers from Cinedrome and calmly drank them in the bar while talking to people, with staff members too busy pouring drinks to complain or prevent us from doing so. I checked my phone for the time. I didn't understand how it was only eleven-thirty p.m. and not four a.m. Going within a short period of time from a high amount of stress to a complete lack of stress after the police had left felt oddly like being on some sort of experimental drug.

Later, around one a.m., I saw Romy at the bar talking to a girl I didn't know. I had lost sight of her after talking to the cops, felt happy she was there but also vaguely anxious, almost anxious by default, as if experiencing a feeling that had been rehearsed so much it had been memorized by my body, could be summoned at any time, like a number on speed dial. I wanted a knob somewhere that I could turn to augment or diminish my self-confidence. There was no knob, but thinking about the knob and then about my self-confidence as something I had control over seemed to help for some reason. I yelled at myself a little in my head. I began to feel like I wanted to be reckless, out-party myself, out-young everyone, get drunk to a point where my decisions weren't decisions anymore, just reflexes.

I went to the bar and approached Romy and her friend. I learned that Romy's friend was named Catherine, and then remembered Catherine from Romy's Facebook Wall. About ten minutes later, Catherine said that she was tired and would be leaving soon. Romy asked me if I was staying and I said, "I think so." After Catherine left, I concentrated on Romy.

"So what happened?" I said. "How come you're back?"

"I was miserable at home," said Romy. "I thought I would get a job there, but I couldn't motivate myself to do anything. I spent way too much time going through Lev's photo albums on Facebook to see pictures of his ex-girlfriend and compare myself to her in my head. She's this very tall, pretty girl who lives in London now."

"It doesn't make for a good comparison," I said. "Like, you're real and she's not. You're a human being with flaws and moods and things and she's this attractive profile picture of herself. You don't think things like, 'Well, maybe she's incredibly self-centered.' It doesn't say that anywhere on her profile."

"I know, but it's also, it doesn't seem like I should be allowed to do this," said Romy. "It's so strange that you can have a Facebook page that's being creeped by some girl you don't even know who exists halfway across the world. Why is that an option?"

Romy laughed nervously.

"Do you feel better, being back?" I said.

"I had a long conversation with my mom and she kept saying, 'You're clearly unhappy,'" said Romy. "So we talked about it and now I am back. I'll be doing summer classes and I'll graduate now instead of in the fall. But I kind of feel like I could be anywhere right now."

We ordered another beer each and then moved from the bar to the back patio. I thought about how we were operating under neutral terms and weren't being anything other than friendly with each other. We sat at a table with Brent, Laura, Cristian and a confident-looking man who introduced himself as "U-Turn." Somehow, Brent and Cristian got into a long, public argument about space travel. Brent was assuming the position of logic and reason while Cristian was referencing things he remembered having read on the internet. Brent mostly wanted Cristian to admit that he was wrong.

"We're never going anywhere," said Brent. "If we go somewhere, it's Mars. We get there, we high-five and then we come back. It's stupid. We're wasting so much money and resources."

"That's because we haven't harnessed electricity in space, that's why space travel sucks right now," said Cristian. "We know a lot about electricity on Earth, but no one talks about electricity in space. Space isn't empty. The material it's made from is technically an electricity conductor, so there might be a way to harness that."

"There's no electricity in space, what are you talking about?" said Brent. "What you're saying doesn't make sense. It's not science."

"I read that on Wikipedia," said Cristian. "It was based on this Russian scientist from the seventies' theories. Or maybe that was the theory itself. I forget. It made a lot of sense."

Every time I looked away and then looked back, the table seemed to have more pitchers of beer on it. I hadn't felt inebriated until now, but was starting to feel less invincible, the proportional amount of drunk. Romy and I weren't really saying anything, just drinking from an endless stream of beer while observing Brent and Cristian go back and forth in an entertaining manner. About twenty minutes later, an employee from Casa walked up to our table and informed us that they would be closing soon and that we would have to leave. Romy asked me what time it was and I said, "It's almost three," and then she made a face and looked more alive and said, "Wait, how am I going to get home?" I asked if she wanted to sleep on the couch and she nodded and I added, "Do you want to go now?" and she said, "Okay."

We got up, explained that we were leaving, said goodbye. Walking, I realized how ruined we both were. Piloting my body felt like piloting a tank. I didn't have a solid grasp on what direction was forward and what direction wasn't. For no concrete reason, I assumed I was less drunk than her and grabbed her hand and then led the way. Holding hands, we walked nonsensically in the general direction of the house, in improvised zigzag patterns and then freestyle patterns. We fell down and laughed and tried getting back up, but then I pushed her down a little and so we fell on the ground again. I thought, "I feel good, minus the drunkenness." Romy was smiling. Around Villeneuve, I stopped and thought, "Do something," and then, "Should I?" and then incomprehensible thoughts that sounded like they were angry at me. I turned around to face her and then moved in quickly and kissed her. While my face was moving towards hers, I saw her mouth placing itself into position. I thought, "I am stupid, she was probably just waiting for me to do that."

Several minutes later, I fell loudly from my bed while taking off my pants.

The next day, I awoke before Romy, with my face facing hers, as if the faces were on a playdate of some sort.

I closed my eyes and lay motionless in the bed. I was naked under the sheets. I felt hungover, as in, "over, my life is over." A few minutes later, Romy awoke, got up, dressed herself before going to the bathroom. Her bra had flower motifs on it. I briefly thought about flower motifs on bras as being a metaphor for something, though couldn't figure out what. Because of the drunkenness, I also wasn't one hundred percent sure we had had sex, though it seemed like we had. While Romy was in the bathroom, I put on a minimum amount of clothing and then checked my phone for the time and saw that it was one p.m. Coming back, Romy saw that I was awake.

"Are you okay?" I said.

"My hair smells like beer," said Romy. She laughed nervously. "I just checked my phone. I had a text from that guy, U-Turn. It just says 'U-Turn' with his phone number."

"When did you exchange phone numbers with him?" I said.

"I have no idea," said Romy. "I am not even sure I talked to him."

"Do you need anything?" I said. "I can offer you cereal, if you want. I don't know what else I have. Probably other things."

"That's fine," said Romy. "What kind of cereal?"

"It's eco-cereal," I said, "with puffins on the box. I don't know if I understand the relationship between the puffins and the cereal."

"I have had that before, the cinnamon one," said Romy. "I think they give money to a foundation that preserves their natural habitats. Or, at least, I hope it's that."

"I wish someone would make a cereal called 'Normal Processed Wheat' and on the box would be factory guys putting wheat in a giant machine," I said.

"I would buy that," said Romy. "Do you have coffee? I would

have that if you have that."

"I have green tea," I said. "Is that okay?"

"That's fine," said Romy.

"Hold on," I said.

I got up and went to the kitchen. We didn't have a kettle, so I filled a pot with water, turned the stove's bottom left burner on, made the water boil by staring at it. A few minutes later, we drank tea in my bed while Romy checked her email and Facebook on my laptop. She read aloud a status update from one of her ex-boyfriend's dad that said "GOLF!!!" along with the name of a country club. She pressed the Like button, which we both thought was funny. She scrolled down a little more and said, "Oh, I like her," and then pressed the Like button again, regardless of what the person's status update said.

"When did you date golf dad's son? When was that?" I said.

"That was right after I moved here," said Romy. "We only dated for a little while. One time, we had sex and he came on my chest. Then he pulled up his pants and said, 'Bye,' and just left. I don't know why I still have his dad on Facebook. I thought I had removed him."

"What does he do now?" I said. "The son. Do you know?"

"I don't know," said Romy. "Has bad sex with girls in dark alleys. He wanted to be an actor, but he was terrible at it. While we were dating, he was doing this play and had to cry on stage. He couldn't get himself to, so he just made agonizing noises instead. It was funny."

"I couldn't do that," I said. "Cry on stage. I would be crying on the inside but not on the outside, and getting angry at people because they can't see it."

"It just takes practice, I think," said Romy.

"Maybe Brent could cast him as an extra in a wedding video," I said. "Making noises in the background, trying to cry."

"I could see that," said Romy. "I thought your roommate was kidding before, when he said that Brent shot wedding videos."

"He only does them when he's screwed for money," I said. "He has a fake production company for them. It's called Perfect Day Studios. There's a trailer on Vimeo. Hold on."

Romy handed me the laptop. I typed something in Google and located the Vimeo account I was looking for. We began watching the trailer for Brent's production company and started laughing about thirty seconds in. In the video, Brent uses overly emotional music and cheap transitions like clockwise wipes and horizontal flips to connect happy moments from different weddings.

"This is so bad," said Romy. "You should show this at your screenings."

"Brent would tear down the screen," I said, "or call the cops himself."

"The only thing I remember from when we were sitting outside last night is Brent yelling at Cristian about outer space," said Romy. "He was really funny."

"Everyone likes Brent," I said.

"Do you get along with him?" said Romy.

"I think so," I said. "I mean, Brent's charismatic and he's proactive and I like that, like it makes me want to keep up with him and put more energy into my own stuff. But he's also kind of an asshole sometimes. He likes to be the moral authority and tell other people what to do. It's like he thinks everyone is really stupid. It's either that, or he's frustrated to be working on little projects instead of a full-length movie or something, so his ego makes him think of himself as a movie director and real life as his movie set. The other day, it was awkward, I heard Laura and him talking in his room. Brent was making fun of me because one time he heard me do intimate things in my room, and that's embarrassing, but it's not the end of the world or something. It was more, like, great, what else are you saying about me behind my back?"

"I hate when that happens," said Romy. "I hear Catherine having sex from time to time. I always think, 'Good for her,' and then, 'Please make it stop.'"

Romy stood up from the bed, mentioned having to leave soon. She located her purse and rummaged through it, at first calmly and then less calmly. She panicked a little and made a face and explained that her wallet was missing. We searched my room, then the house, couldn't find it. I said, "Do you think you left it at Casa?" and Romy replied that she didn't know. She seemed anxious. "Let's just go there right now," I said. "They probably have a lost and found." We left the house and walked to the bar. On the way there, I tried making small talk and introducing new conversation topics, but Romy suddenly seemed more distant, less talkative. "She's probably just concerned," I thought. A few minutes later, we entered Casa. Romy explained her situation to the only employee present and then described the wallet as "brown" and made from "not leather." The employee said, "Hold on," and went to look for it in the back and returned with a wallet. "Is this it?" the employee said. Romy said, "Yes, thank you," and then, "Thank you" a second time. She placed her wallet back in her purse, seemed relieved.

"That was a lot of drama for nothing," said Romy.

"How did you lose it in the first place? You don't remember?" I said.

"I am starting to think I just forgot it on the counter after ordering a beer," said Romy. "That sounds like me."

"Is anything missing?" I said.

"I don't think so," said Romy, "or doesn't seem to be. What would be the closest metro station from here?"

"I'll walk you," I said.

"You don't have to," said Romy.

"I don't mind," I said. "Come on."

Exiting the bar, we headed in the direction of the Laurier station. Sunlight was hitting my face, requiring a kind of effort I wasn't sure I wanted to be making. Though we had found her wallet, Romy was still being mostly quiet. I thought, "If I have to do most of the talking, we're in trouble." The farther away we were getting from the bed, the more we seemed to be going back to operating under neutral terms with each other. It was as if we had slept together, but both decided not to tell the other person.

Later, as we said goodbye, we hugged, but didn't kiss.

A combination of rain and wind knocked the Cinedrome screen to the ground, damaging it in the process. Brent was able to fix it, but the screen looked as though it could fall apart at any moment. "I don't think it's going to make it through another winter," said Brent.

I couldn't tell if I had a good understanding of who Romy was or if I was just projecting what I thought I desired onto her, to a point where there was barely anything of her left.

I usually tossed letters addressed to previous tenants or to no one in particular into a pile on a small table near the front door. The pile had taken over the entire table, was starting to look threatening.

"I think we're about to be downsized," said Sebastian. I was searching the office kitchen's drawers for a plastic fork and overheard people gossiping. "They give us all these shitty licenses and then they blame us when we don't make as much money as they wanted us to make. It's so stupid. We're set up to fail." The studio being downsized likely meant that a number of employees would be let go, though I didn't seem to be too concerned about this. I just thought it was funny how I wasn't really talking with anyone anymore, but was still aware of most of the rumours.

My confidence level was always a wild card.

Coming back home, I found on the kitchen table six post-dated cheques signed by Ines next to a note that said "Rent stuff," along with my name in pretty handwriting and an arrow pointing to the cheques.

"Well, in *Shadow of the Colossus*," said Todd, who was also a game designer. I was still showing up to meetings at work, though had stopped pretending I had a positive attitude, which was an improvement. Todd was a slightly chubby man in his early thirties who often wore a plaid hat and seemed self-assured. His favourite video game was *Shadow of the Colossus*. In the game, a young man seeking to rehabilitate a loved one is tasked by an ancient spirit to locate and slay sixteen massive creatures roaming a barren and desolate wasteland. I disliked Todd. I didn't understand how society hadn't destroyed this person's self-confidence. I didn't understand how anyone had self-confidence, seeing how we were constantly with ourselves, constantly accumulating dirt on ourselves, constantly witnessing our own flaws, humiliations, defeats.

I sent Romy a text message asking if she was coming over for Cinedrome and then waited. It was the second Friday of July. An hour passed and then more hours passed. I had wanted to let a few days go by before messaging her, maybe use an emoticon in the message like a wink or a grin, but somehow that had turned into waiting an entire week to contact her.

I had given up on seeing Romy and had made other plans in my head when I received a response from her. We exchanged messages and arranged to meet. Later, around one-thirty a.m., we found each other on the sidewalk in front of Blizzarts, near the window. Romy was talking to Shannon, who was wearing silver shorts and an old Nirvana t-shirt. Shannon hugged me and kissed me briefly on the cheek. Then I hugged Romy and kissed her on the head like a newborn. Shannon was usually the one who initiated hugs, didn't want to let go, made the hug feel as if it had some sort of five-act structure, like a play. Being hugged by Shannon felt like being defeated by a superior opponent, but learning in the process. With Romy, I had to be the one who imposed the hug. Transitioning out of the hug with her, a part of me wanted to think, "I'll teach you."

Judging from the number of people on the sidewalk, being outside the club seemed preferable to being inside the club. "You're coming to my little diner party on Tuesday, right?" said Shannon. I confirmed I was. Less than a minute later, Shannon spotted someone else she knew, became agitated, left to go hug the person. I turned to Romy.

"How was your week?" I said.

"I only realized this when I got home," said Romy, "but I am pretty sure someone stole a twenty from my wallet, unless I drank it and don't remember."

"It's probably better to presume you drank it," I said.

"I think so too," said Romy. "My week was normal other than that. I went to a job interview today, from this Craigslist ad. I didn't know where it was, but it was actually really far up north. It was this small office, they sell a special brand of car wax. They showed us an infomercial video on how to apply the wax. They didn't specify what the position was and I felt too embarrassed to ask, like I think I was supposed to know before going in. I kept trying to guess. Am I calling people on the phone and trying to sell products to them? Do they want me to do car shows and apply the wax side-to-side like the guy in the infomercial? Is that why they're showing us the video? I didn't understand. Then a nice lady interviewed me for about half an hour, but she only asked me basic questions."

"What did she ask you?" I said.

"Like, 'Where do you see yourself in five years?' " said Romy. "I just wanted to say, 'Not here. I don't even know where I am.' "

"So what was the position, do you know?" I said.

"I still don't know," said Romy. She laughed nervously. "They asked me to come in for a second interview, though."

"That's funny," I said.

"I am not sure I'll go," said Romy. "I think I'll decide on Monday."

Romy abruptly changed conversation topics, mentioned that Shannon had told her about an after-party we could go to later. Then she asked if I could find "party help." She explained that she didn't do drugs very often and still felt shy about asking around for them. "It shouldn't be impossible," I said.

I wondered if she thought I was a generic, bullshit cool person that knows what he's doing and has a dealer and self-confidence. I still couldn't decide if I wanted her to think that or not. I told Romy I would "ask around" and then scanned the crowd, trying to spot someone sketchy-looking. Everyone around me looked about the same sketchiness level. I approached a person at random and explained what I wanted and said, "party help" instead of "drugs."

The person replied, "Sorry, bro."

I thought, "Even if they had anything, they wouldn't sell to me."

I didn't want to go back to Romy empty-handed, but wasn't sure who to ask next. I stalled for about thirty seconds and then spotted JJ across the street, coming out of a pizza place and wearing the same hoodie as the night we had met. I crossed the street despite traffic and then went up to him and said, "Hey." JJ seemed to remember me, shook my hand, asked how I was. I said, "I am good." I explained what I was looking for and he replied that all he had on him were two MDMA pills, but that he was willing to sell them to me. I thought a brief succession of positive statements. I imagined the Hollywood sign spelling "SUCCESS" instead of "HOLLYWOOD." JJ named a price and we proceeded with the exchange. He said, "Have a good night," politely, before leaving.

I crossed the street again, went back to Romy, felt surprised by my failure to fail.

About an hour later, Romy, Shannon and I walked up a deserted street and then stopped in front of a white building made of concrete. "It's here," said Shannon. We went down to the basement. A sign near the door said "Five dollars to get in." We were stamped in and looked around and saw that the space was only a quarter full and not particularly interesting. The venue looked like an abandoned laundromat. "I guess it's still early for this," said Shannon. "The bars are going to close soon. It'll fill up after that. We should try again later."

We purchased a beer each and decided to go back outside to kill time. We looked around for a quiet place to hang out and found an alley overseen by tall, hyperventilating industrial buildings. We sat on the ground, drank our beers.

Romy and I swallowed a pill of MDMA each.

"I've never actually done MDMA," said Romy.

"Usually, all that happens is that I am more enthusiastic about things and feel good about everyone," I said. "Like, if I am talking to someone, I'll be really into it, even it's someone I wouldn't normally find interesting."

"Have you ever had MDMA dreams?" said Shannon.

"What do you mean?" I said.

"There's a bunch of times where I did MDMA and had these crazy dreams with shapes and bright colours flashing," said Shannon, "like a rave or a Japanese cartoon."

"I don't think I've had those," I said.

"Maybe tonight," said Shannon.

Glancing at Romy, I noticed that she seemed a little bored. Shannon took control of the conversation, mostly talking about herself. I paid half-attention to what Shannon was saying, imagining in my head a Japanese cartoon about giant robots going to raves and feeling trapped by their lifestyles. I tuned back in just as Shannon started talking about an essay by Camille Roy she had read recently. Paraphrasing the essay, she said it argued that most mainstream novels observed their characters from a medium distance and treated them as coherent human beings elevated by conflict as opposed to destroyed by it. I thought, "Coherent human being," and couldn't think of anyone I knew who fit this description.

An unknown amount of time later, we got up, headed back in. Walking, Romy lost her balance a few times, but didn't fall down. Entering the space, I saw that the venue was now about half full. I examined the crowd to see if anyone I knew was there, but then lost track of Shannon. The MDMA pill I had ingested didn't seem to be having any effect, while the beers I had drunk only seemed to be having a little effect. Looking back at Romy, I noticed that she had difficulty standing still and was now smiling a sort of dumb smile.

"Is Lev here?" said Romy.

"Probably not," I said. "Isn't he in New York?"

"Lev looks like a Viking," said Romy.

"He would be easy to spot, then," I said.

"If there's anything, I'll be Lev," said Romy.

"What do you mean?" I said.

"I can't," said Romy. "So I am never both been the same."

I wasn't sure what she was trying to tell me. I looked directly at her and saw that she looked out of it a little. I said, "Are you okay?" and she replied, "I am fine, but never is." I began to feel concerned. I asked if she was okay again, but she was having trouble putting together complete sentences. She said, "Lev," and, "I can't," aloud to herself a few times. "I've been more decided," she said. "The point is, I am more decided." She was making less and less sense, as if a lingual module in her brain was toggling back and forth between Canadian English and Malaysian, like a keyboard.

I thought, "What happened, she was fine in the alley, I think, when did she get this drunk, I am pretty sure I drank more than her, how is she drunker than me?"

I felt jealous a little.

Romy moved towards me and then managed to put a sentence together. "I don't want to be here anymore," she said. "Can we go to bed?" I thought about the bed as a happy place and said yes.

I grabbed her hand, didn't bother tracking down Shannon to say goodbye, led us to the exit. Outside, Romy seemed unable to walk by herself. I was still puzzled by how she had gotten to this state. She seemed to be getting worse and worse, as if going through a night of serious drinking on fast-forward. I knew it would be easier to signal for a cab on St-Laurent, so I grabbed her purse and lifted her and then carried her in my arms. I noticed that she wasn't saying anything anymore, just babbling experimental noises, like a one-year-old. She wasn't particularly heavy, but I had to stop twice to allow my arms to recuperate. I thought, "This is why people work out, I see the value of working out now." I kept readjusting her position in my arms, as if hoping to find on her body a grip or a handle of some sort.

I didn't find one.

Romy threw up on me a little.

Near St-Laurent, I placed Romy on the ground and waved at cabs. I looked back in her direction and saw that she was now semi-conscious, her eyes half-open and pointing upwards, as if her eyeballs were trying to perform some sort of retinal backflip. I wasn't sure what to do, but for some reason wasn't panicking too much. A cab stopped on the side of the road. The driver asked me if Romy was okay. I didn't respond and instead, reached for my phone, called an ambulance. Other passersby saw Romy on the ground and then surrounded her and patted her head and tried giving her water. The right strap of Romy's tank top kept falling down, exposing her boob and then not exposing it and then exposing it again. Some people shouted contradictory advice at one another. One person tried to dissuade me from calling an ambulance, because ambulances were costly and Romy would be mad at me later for requesting one. Someone else said that she was clenching her jaw and then asked me if she had done heroin and I replied, "No."

About ten minutes later, an ambulance arrived. While his colleague examined Romy, the driver interrogated me.

"What happened here?" said the driver.

"I don't know," I said. "She started acting strange, then she just fainted."

"Did she fall down?" said the driver. "Did she knock her head?"

"No, I was the one who placed her on the ground," I said.

"I am guessing she was drinking," said the driver. "Has she taken anything else?"

"Not that I know of, but I wasn't with her the entire time," I said. I was lying.

I answered a few more questions, but then became aware that the MDMA pill I had taken earlier was finally kicking in a little. I felt, all at once, drug-happy and concerned for Romy and very tired. I avoided telling the driver about our drug use and kept a straight face, but could hear myself inside my head giggling from a safe distance.

The MDMA was making me very interested in my conversation with the driver.

"Are you coming with us?" the driver's colleague asked me a few minutes later. I replied, "Yes," loudly and enthusiastically.

"Calm down," I thought. "You're enjoying this too much."

"Drugs," I thought.

"We're leaving now," said the driver's colleague. "Get in."

I opened the passenger door of the ambulance and climbed in. On the way to the hospital, I decided to avoid talking altogether, for fear of appearing suspicious. Instead, I focused on the movements of the rear lights of the car ahead of us, thought thoughts in silence.

In the parking lot, the driver and the driver's colleague wheeled Romy towards the entrance. I thought about how I was already starting to feel the MDMA less and less. Exiting an elevator, we stopped at a station. A nurse asked me for Romy's ID card and medicare card. I had her purse with me, so I browsed through it at random and found lip balm and then a pamphlet about stress titled, "What Do You Know About Stress?"

I felt stressed a little, staring at the pamphlet about stress.

I located her wallet and then, inside it, her driver's license. Staring at the license, I saw that her full name was Rosemary and not Romy and that her middle name was Louise. I made a face. The nurse asked me if Romy had an emergency contact number and I said, "I don't know," and she said, "But you're her boyfriend." I paused. I felt like I wanted to use this opportunity to discuss my relationship with Romy with the nurse, maybe ask her for guidance or life advice, but instead said, "Yeah," in a tone that lacked confidence.

While the nurse was processing the driver's license, Romy regained consciousness. She opened her eyes and mouth and made a face as if getting ready to make a dramatic gasp for air, the way actors in movies emerge from comas, but then didn't. She babbled nonsense for a few minutes and began putting together sentences and thoughts. In a calm voice, I explained to her what had happened, though I wasn't sure she understood what I was telling her. She looked disoriented and seemed to be having short-term memory issues. She asked me several times, "Are you staying with me? Don't go," and I said, "I am staying, don't worry," each time. She requested Lev again.

A male nurse, Michel, introduced himself to us. Romy said, "What's up?" to him, as if wanting to be his friend a little. The male nurse had long golden floppy hair, like a cocker spaniel. He wheeled Romy to a different room and then transferred her into a bed. He started removing her clothes to change her into a gown, which made Romy anxious and uncomfortable. She made a face. She looked scared and lost and clutched my arm like a robot grip crushing a beer can, and then panicked a little and shouted, "Don't let them put things in my vagina." I said, "Don't worry, I'll bodyguard your vagina."

This seemed to make her less anxious.

Since there was nowhere to sit, I stood beside Romy's bed. Around us were multiple beds, though only one was occupied, by an old woman who looked horrified in her sleep. The male nurse checked Romy's heart rate and then informed us that a doctor would be coming to see her, though this might take several hours. We waited. For about an hour, Romy tried resting, but couldn't fall asleep. She said, "I am fucked," two or three times. She asked for more details about what had happened and I said that we were at a sketchy after-party and that she had had a bad reaction to drugs. Looking out the window, I became aware that the sun was about to rise. Another hour passed. Romy seemed to be doing better, didn't have memory issues anymore. We both felt alienated from the hospital itself and wanted to leave, but couldn't. The male nurse wheeled in a new patient, a man in maybe his late forties wearing a shirt with an eagle on it and a cowboy hat made from what appeared to be snakeskin. Another man, wearing an orange shirt, was accompanying him.

"Let me get your hat for you, Roger," said the man in the orange shirt in French. He seemed either emotionally invested in his friend or emotionally invested in the hat.

"Do you think they're lovers?" said Romy.

"I don't know," I said. "The other guy could be pretending. He could be into it just for the hat."

"You're right," said Romy. "It's a beautiful hat. A snake died to make that hat."

"I want to be turned into a hat when I die," I said. "There has to be a box somewhere I can check for that, like organ donor."

"There should be," said Romy. "My dad told us that he wanted to be cremated after he dies, and then for one of us to toss his ashes into the wind, so that he becomes the wind. He thinks it's romantic. I think his ashes will probably just end up killing seagulls."

"Have you ever been to Texas with your dad?" I said.

"Wait," said Romy. "Are you okay?"

"I am fine," I said. "It's just, there's nowhere for me to sit, so my legs are getting cramped."

"Climb in," said Romy.

"Are you sure?" I said. "It's a tiny hospital bed."

"It'll be funny," said Romy. "Come on."

She tapped on the mattress with her hand. I said, "Okay," took off my shoes, climbed in the bed. She shifted to her right and we got into position. The bed was clearly too small to accommodate both our bodies, but we shared the space and began conversing inches away from one another's face while laughing.

"I've been to Texas a couple of times," said Romy. "My grandma, my dad's mom, is ninety-four, but she's still sharp and witty. She kept dissing my dad when we were there. It was great."

"Did you get along with her?" I said.

"I liked her," said Romy. "The last time I was there, she kept telling me about all her old boyfriends. It was strange. If she didn't forget anyone, my boyfriend graveyard is the same size as hers. She was really nice to me. I think she just likes me because my middle name is her name."

"Louise," I said.

"Yeah," said Romy. "How do you know that?"

"Your real name is Rosemary," I said. "I didn't even know that. The nurse asked me for your ID, so I looked through your purse and found your driver's license. I just looked at it and it was like, 'Who the fuck is Rosemary?'"

"A very special person," said Romy.

"The nurse asked me if we were together," I said.

"Do you mean married?" said Romy.

"No, I just meant, like, dating," I said.

"What did you say?" said Romy.

"I said yes just because it was simpler," I said.

"You should have told her we were married," said Romy, "and that the sketchy after-party was our ten-year wedding anniversary."

"Shit," I said. "Next time."

"Our babies would be so white," said Romy. She laughed nervously.

"Our babies would get emails from me all the time telling them how I feel," I said. "They would block me after a while."

"Probably," said Romy.

She laughed. We stared at each other for a few seconds, but didn't say anything. We kissed, then stopped and stared at each other again for several seconds. I heard someone walking in the room. I looked and saw a man in a lab coat heading in our direction. I got up.

"Hello," said the man. He looked about forty, had a trimmed moustache, round glasses. He glanced at his clipboard. "Romy. Hi."

The man, Dr. Carpentier, introduced himself and asked Romy various questions about her current physical and mental condition. As she answered, he nodded in agreement, seemed satisfied with her progress.

"So," said the doctor. "We found an unknown substance in your blood. Do you have any idea where it came from? Anything you might have taken?"

"I don't remember," said Romy.

"Do you?" said the doctor to me.

"I wasn't with her the entire time," I said. "Not to my knowledge, but someone could have put something in her drink."

The doctor didn't seem convinced by my lie. He cautioned us against being reckless and partying. While he was lecturing us, I thought about having lied to him just now and kind of wanted to rewind back in time a little, like in a video game, tell him we had purchased MDMA pills from a polite drug dealer and ingested them in an alley, see how he reacts, if that really changes anything.

Romy was discharged and told she could leave. As she was getting dressed, she said, "I hate hospitals." I asked if she wanted to steal something while we were here, as revenge, and instead of replying, she grabbed a Styrofoam cup and a small white and blue object made of plastic from the shelf in front of her. Waiting for the elevator, I examined the object and wasn't sure what its function was, if any. It looked like a laser pointer whose signal could only be seen by bats or dolphins.

Outside, we crossed the street and signalled for a cab. We weren't saying anything, but for once the silence didn't feel anxiety-filled or death-defying. We cabbed to the corner of Mont-Royal and St-Laurent and tipped the driver all we had left, which was a quarter, a dime, some pennies, the Styrofoam cup and the pointer. It was now Saturday morning. The streets were empty, except for strange people exploring garbage bins for beer bottles and cans with surprising stamina and speed. We passed by the garage door with the graffiti that said "Ghostbusters" on it and I said, "Wait," and reached for my phone. I photographed Romy smiling next to the graffiti, with bed hair that randomly looked excellent.

Back at the house, we went directly to my room and then collapsed in my bed. I fell asleep holding Romy, but then awoke in a sweat maybe two hours later. I still felt exhausted, but my body wanted me to be up for some reason. Trying to avoid disturbing Romy, I grabbed my laptop, moved to the kitchen, made tea, checked websites. Then I closed the web browser and opened a word processor. I began noting down everything I remembered from the previous twelve hours. I didn't have a good reason for writing down what had happened other than being affected by it and wanting to remember feeling close to Romy. I thought about an article I had read in a magazine a few years before that said communities that endured horrible tragedies like a massive earthquake or a killing flood often felt closer and more united in the aftermath.

I wrote for a few hours. Then I heard sounds coming from my room, saw Romy walking out. She sat on the couch in the common area, seemed dizzy a little.

"How do you feel?" I said. "Do you want water?"

"Maybe, yeah," said Romy. "I feel half-fucked, half-okay."

I opened a cupboard and reached for a glass, but then remembered that all we had were wine glasses and assorted mugs. I poured water into a wine glass.

"We don't have normal glasses," I said. "Just these."

"That's fine," said Romy.

"Did you have anything planned today?" I said.

"Not really," said Romy. "I have the car wax interview on Monday and then that dinner at Shannon's on Tuesday night. And my summer classes. That's pretty much it. I think I'll go home and rest."

"Do you want me to call you a cab?" I said.

"I don't have money," said Romy.

"I'll pay for it, I don't care," I said.

"You don't have to," said Romy. "I could find an ATM or something."

"It's okay," I said. "Hold on."

I went to my room and came back with a twenty-dollar bill and handed it to her. We went back and forth a little about her taking the money, but I insisted and was able to convince her. I accompanied her out and said, "Are you going to be okay?" and she said, "I think so." We talked about seeing each other on Tuesday.

As we said goodbye, I kissed her quickly on the lips. She seemed surprised by the kiss, but didn't say anything.

"She should be okay," I typed to Shannon on Facebook Chat. "She wasn't in danger or anything, it was just ugly for a while. What's strange is that I ingested the same thing as her and I was fine."

"She's so tiny, though," typed Shannon. "She's like 5' 1". It could have been too much for her."

"You've seen people get really trashed at parties, right?" I typed.

"Yeah," typed Shannon. "People going into k-holes or losing their shit. All kinds of things."

"Have you ever seen anything like that happen?" I typed.

"From just one pill of MDMA," typed Shannon. "No, never."

"That was bad," I typed.

"It was good for your little romance, though," typed Shannon.

"I don't know," I typed. "I mean, I ended up poisoning her. That's probably not romantic."

"Didn't you guys sleep together?" typed Shannon.

"Technically, yes," I typed. "But it didn't seem like a big deal to her."

"It still happened," typed Shannon.

"At the hospital, she was asking for Lev a lot," I typed.

"Is that the guy she was seeing before?" typed Shannon. "I don't think I know him."

"But you know everyone," I typed.

"I know, that doesn't make any sense," typed Shannon. "Where is this person I've never met hiding? We should stalk him."

"Should we?" I typed. "She probably has him in her friends list."

"We're stalking him," typed Shannon.

About thirty seconds later, Shannon copy-pasted a link to Lev's Facebook account in the Chat window. In his profile picture, he had a short beard and long hair and seemed tall and was wearing a button-down dress shirt. He looked like more of a dad than I ever would.

"Shit," I typed. "He's handsome."

"I don't know if I would call him handsome," typed Shannon. "But he's manly."

"I am fucked," I typed. "That didn't help at all."

"I just wanted to thank you for what you did for Romy," said a voice-mail from Catherine on my phone.

I thought about my true motivation for doing drugs, which was probably to distance myself from my anxieties. I thought about Brent's true motivation for doing drugs, which was probably to dumb himself down to everyone else's level. I thought about Shannon's true motivation for doing drugs, which was probably to want everything, even though everything wouldn't be enough.

"He lives his life in $1,000 increments," read Brent's Facebook status. "He is. The freelancer."

I climbed the stairs to Shannon's apartment. It was Tuesday. I took off my shoes, overheard multiple voices, walked in the direction of the kitchen. "Baby," Shannon said excitedly. She was wearing a green dress with tiny cut-outs on the side, gold sandals, oversized earrings large enough for a hamster to jump through. I saw Romy from afar, talking to someone on the porch, but decided not to go to her for now. I sat in the living room and socialized with Shannon and some of her friends. Around us were leather couches facing one another, a chandelier, unlit candles, a glass table, a tall bookcase and a Bettie Page poster in which Bettie Page was wearing lingerie while on fire.

I drank beers.

One of the friends was named Paul and was a DJ and also played in a band called Burnaby Rebellion. I asked Paul why the band was called Burnaby Rebellion and he replied that two members of the band were from Burnaby in British Columbia and disliked the city.

Later, Shannon said, "If we're out on a date, this is bad. That probably means I don't like you, because otherwise, I would just sleep with you."

Later, because of my French accent coming out, I had difficulty pronouncing the word "alley-oop" properly and was made fun of a little.

Later, I scanned the homemade buffet on Shannon's dinner table. There was a large fruit salad, roasted tofu, pasta salad, unidentified salads, about ten different desserts, other food items. I said hi to Romy, who was now in the same room as me, and briefly chatted with her. "She seems indifferent about me being here," I thought. Then someone else arrived, creating a distraction that prevented me from getting a deeper conversation going. I lost sight of Romy for about half an hour and then saw her grabbing her purse and remaining beers. She thanked Shannon for having her and then explained that she had to go.

"Are you leaving?" I said.

"Yeah, there's somewhere else I have to be," said Romy. "Oh wait, I have something for you."

She smiled, rummaged through her purse, pulled out the stress pamphlet, continued digging. At the bottom of her purse, she found a twenty-dollar bill and handed it to me.

"Thank you," I said.

"No, thank you for paying for the cab," said Romy.

"Were you okay on Saturday?" I said.

"I am fine now," said Romy. "I didn't go to that interview. It was at eleven a.m. and I woke up at two p.m. It was like, 'Well, I guess I decided not to go.' Catherine had friends over on Sunday. I thought I was okay, but then I started feeling woozy and couldn't talk to anyone anymore. After a while, I said, 'I have to go,' and went to hide in my room. They must have thought, 'What's wrong with this girl?'"

"At the hospital, I don't know if you remember that part, but you said, 'What's up?' to the male nurse," I said. "He looked at you funny, like he was thinking, 'What's wrong with this girl?'"

"I honestly don't remember most of what happened," said Romy. "I remember Blizzarts and waking up in your room, but everything in between is like death metal music."

"I don't know if I should tell you this," I said, "but while you were sleeping, I got up and wrote down everything I remembered from the hospital. I just didn't want to forget it. I know there's probably sensitive stuff for you in there, so I am not going to put that online or something. I could send it to you if you want. It's not that long."

"Should I read it?" said Romy.

"I don't know," I said. "I am not sure how you would react to it."

"Okay," said Romy. "Well, send it to me by email if you want. Do you remember, at the hospital, them saying anything about the bill for the ambulance? I called and spoke to a receptionist, but it was confusing. I don't want any kind of bill showing up at my parents' house."

"They took your driver's license," I said. "If that's the address on it, they'll probably send it there."

"Shit," said Romy. "I'll try calling the hospital again."

Romy mentioned that she had to go a second time and then we said goodbye in a neutral, friendly manner.

I was now coming in late to work almost every day. My strategy was to rush whatever tasks I had, to get rid of them as fast as possible and write poems for the rest of the day. Julian was assigning me fewer and fewer tasks outside of the work I did on Scrabble. Though we hadn't talked about it, I felt like he was disappointed in me and had lost confidence in me, which I decided to view as something positive. Writing poems at the office was also making work more interesting. I hadn't been authorized by anyone to do this and had to watch out for Carl, who sometimes looked over my shoulder and observed me working. If I had a word processor opened and a graph onscreen, it usually looked to him like I was being productive. I kept thinking that maybe what I wanted to happen was to get caught by someone.

I edited my notes from the hospital before sending them to Romy. My only major change was to remove all mentions of Lev, her asking for him.

"There's this girl that's been texting me," said Cristian. "She sounds like what I sound like when I am texting girls. 'Hey, what are you doing? Want to hang out?' It's confusing. It's like, if you're me, am I you? What's my role then? What am I supposed to be doing? Not texting her back, I guess."

On Facebook, I saw that Brent had shared a link to the final edit of the music video that featured Cristian and Kyle. I watched it and shared it on my Wall, but wasn't sure I liked it. Brent's lack of patience showed, with quick cuts and sloppy transitions. In the description box, he had written an overly serious synopsis, specifying that the use of the colour red in the video represented danger, while blue represented healing and green represented life and rebirth, as if using symbols automatically transformed something into "art."

Hungover, I sat in the conference room and drank water from my company mug with a company logo on it and then stared blankly at Sebastian's company mug with a faded company logo on it. Up on screen were 3D pipes assembling themselves. Julian entered the room, closing the door behind him.

"Gentleman," said Julian. Noticing the pipes, he stopped, made a face and then an annoyed grunt. "God, why can't anyone ever remember to log out?"

He walked to the conference table, took control of the mouse and keyboard, which replaced the pipes with a generic Windows desktop. Julian browsed through sub-menus, trying to log out. While waiting, I glanced at my surroundings. On the conference table in front of me, it seemed like there were more coffee mugs than there were people, as if some employees had brought more than one with them.

"Okay, here we go," said Julian. "Hi. Sorry about this. Welcome to today's game design meeting."

Every once a while, the studio's designers gathered in the conference room to discuss video games from a design perspective. The goal of this was to further everyone's understanding of various game design principles. I didn't think of these meetings as particularly useful, because we almost never designed games for ourselves. Instead, we designed games for users who were the polar opposite of ourselves, who, in theory, rarely played video games and wanted to be told exactly what to do and how do it. Since we spent our days protected from the outside world, locked in an office and forced to repeat different variations of the same events, it was hard to imagine who these abstract users who played our games were. Forty-year-old housewives? Karate instructors wearing combat pyjamas, bored and waiting for the bus? An alien sitting at a shiny and curvilinear work desk, seeking escape from the disappointing reality of having to fire red beams at Mayan temples?

"The topic of today's meeting," said Julian, "is Stuff vs. Fluff. What do you consider fluff? What do you consider stuff? By stuff, I mean the core elements of a game. Without them, you have nothing. By fluff, I mean extra features that could be cut and your game would still technically hold together. But would it be any fun? How important is fluff? Anyone want to comment?"

Todd quickly raised his hand while everyone else in the room remained silent.

"Go ahead," said Julian.

"The true beauty of *Shadow of the Colossus*," said Todd, "is that there is no fluff. Every moment is essential. Every move, every sound, every little piece of dialogue, everything. Even the controls have no fluff. Take the grabbing mechanic. You have to hold down the R1 button for the main character to hold onto a ledge. You don't just press R1, you have to hold it. It's subtle. As soon as you let go, the main character also lets go. The player and the character are never dissociated from one another. You feel for the character because you are the character."

"Right," said Julian.

"To me, fluff in first-person shooters," said Sebastian, "is always the tutorial that teaches you basic game mechanics you could have figured out on your own. But then, is that fluff? Or would people be lost if there was no tutorial?"

"Great question," said Julian. "Are tutorials fluff? What can we do to make tutorials feel more essential? Should a tutorial be as fun as the game itself?"

Todd raised his hand again.

"Let's go around the table and try someone new first," said Julian. "Thomas, we haven't heard much from you lately. Any thoughts?"

I didn't have any thoughts.

"I don't know," I said. "I mean, even if we decided to remove everything that we consider fluff, there would probably be someone above us telling us to put it back in."

"Well, you have to accept that that's just part of the process," said Julian.

"That's the problem," I said.

"We should make a game that's fluff only," said Sebastian.

"That's all our games," said Todd.

Most people in the room laughed.

No one had told the rain that it wasn't supposed to rain. On his laptop, Brent composed a message addressed to everyone attending our Facebook event, letting them know that this week's Cinedrome would be cancelled. It was the last Friday of July. We sat in the common area and stared at the cases of Pabst Blue Ribbon that Cristian had bought two hours before. The cases stared back at us.

"Should we save them for next week?" said Cristian.

"If we can," said Brent. He grabbed one of the cases, opened it, handed a can to Cristian and me and then kept one for himself.

"I don't think they'll last a week," said Cristian.

"Probably not," said Brent.

We drank beers and talked for a while, waiting for the rain to grow bored, fade itself out. Friends of Brent showed up despite the weather and then stayed because we offered them free alcohol. "Two months after I moved here, I saw Alex playing in someone's kitchen," said Brent to everyone, "and now two years later, they're playing Sala Rossa with four keyboards and this ridiculous fake jungle set behind them. When people talk about the music scene here, that's always the first thing they miss. Musicians don't come out of nowhere. People come here because education is cheap and then they stay because they can play in small venues like lofts or jam spaces or someone's apartment or whatever, and get better at what they're doing. It's not even hard to put stuff together. It's always like, oh, I know this guy, we can use his space, then I'll ask these guys to play, then I'll pick the stupidest picture I can think of for the Facebook event, and that's it, done. You don't need money, you need people. It's not money that's the currency here. It's who you know."

Around ten-thirty, the rain slowed down and then stopped. The stack of empty beer cans on the ground was now forming a castle-like structure. I exchanged texts with Romy and Shannon and then convinced myself to head down to Saint-Henri. Getting my bike, I saw Cristian's leaning against a wall. I thought, "Dead kid." I imagined getting hit by multiple cars, someone putting together an effigy in the backyard in my honour, then Cristian stealing my bike from the effigy. I decided to use public transport instead. I transferred beers into my backpack, said goodbye, left the house. On my way to the metro station, I sent another text to Romy. I kind of wanted to follow the text to its destination, going from my phone to Romy's phone, but then thought about this in too much detail and imagined my body being relayed to a satellite in outer space and then sent back to Earth, burning during re-entry and crashing like a comet.

While waiting for the metro at Mont-Royal, I read passages at random from *Speedboat* by Renata Adler. I got in, rode for about twenty minutes, didn't pay attention to people around me, got out at Lionel-Groulx. Outside, I walked for a few streets and then easily located the address Shannon had sent me. I entered the space with an unexpected amount of self-confidence, though it felt more like a mirage pretending to be a real thing than a real thing. Around me were tall vertical windows, wooden floors, a large open area, a laptop connected to large speakers playing what sounded like warped house music, a smoke machine.

The crowd looked like it had been cloned from another house party.

I went outside to escape the smoke and found Romy on the back porch. She was wearing a white polo with a yellow collar and a small bunny sewn on the pocket, a skirt with flower motifs on it and dark purple leggings. In the back, I saw Shannon talking to someone else.

"It's so much better out here," I said.

"I know," said Romy. "I stayed inside for five minutes and said hi to Daniel and that was already too much."

"Where did you get the bunny shirt?" I said.

"I bought it at a yard sale a year ago," said Romy. "I didn't know what to wear tonight. I tried on clothes like a girl for forty-five minutes and then at some point my brain made this. I look like a Pokémon."

Romy laughed nervously.

"No, it's good," I said.

"Do you remember U-Turn?" said Romy. "I still have his

number. I tried texting him to see if he had weed earlier. He texted back that he would trade me some for a massage."

"What did you tell him?" I said.

"I didn't reply," said Romy. "What do you reply do that?"

"You should have told him, 'I know a special place for those,' and then given him the address of the car wax place," I said.

Romy laughed a little. I thought about how she felt not too close, but not too far either. "Medium distance," I thought.

"It's good to know that I can always fall back on starting a massage-for-weed business," said Romy.

"Work from home," I said.

"The ambulance bill showed up at my parents' house," said Romy. "I had to explain what happened. I told them it was alcohol poisoning. I couldn't tell if they bought that or not. They're going to pay for it, but only because they get to yell at me and tell me that I am a fuck up."

"I didn't know that was going to happen," I said.

"You should have asked more clearly," said Romy. "About the bill, I mean. Like where they were going to send it."

"Wait, are you mad at me?" I said.

"No, not really," said Romy. "I mean, I just feel strange about everything that happened. I looked at the notes you emailed me. It was kind of disturbing to read about what I had done. It was like on TV when they show people videos of themselves under hypnosis."

"I hesitated before sending them to you," I said. "I wasn't sure if I should."

"No, I wanted to read them," said Romy. "Thank you."

From a side angle, I saw Shannon approaching us. She wasn't smiling, didn't look overexcited, hugged neither Romy nor me, just stood beside us neutrally, as if next to someone on the bus.

"Thank god you guys are here," said Shannon.

"Are you okay?" I said.

"I am all right," said Shannon. "I was so happy on Tuesday."

"I liked Tuesday," I said.

"Me too, but then I went out on Wednesday and it was horrible," said Shannon. "I have been having strong need-to-go-somewhere feelings ever since. You know when you just feel like you should be somewhere else, briefly, for perspective?"

"I know what you mean," I said. "Shit's too real, escape somewhere else."

"That's the problem," said Shannon. "Shit's not real enough right now."

"Shit not being real enough is still 'shit being too real,' " I said.

"I just want something new to happen," said Shannon, "but something that made sense all along, in hindsight. I don't know what I am saying."

"What would make you feel better right now?" said Romy.

"Something drastic," said Shannon. "Earlier, Daniel was like, 'I should give you a haircut, we could shave your side, all the way up.' Something like that."

"I didn't know Daniel cut hair," said Romy.

"I think he likes to give people drunk haircuts," said Shannon. "I was there the other day when he did it to his roommate. If he's just shaving my left side, it's not that hard, it can't be a disaster."

"I would get a haircut if you got one," I said.

"You would?" said Shannon.

"I think so," I said.

"Let's go ask Daniel," said Shannon. "I don't even care if it's a disaster. I want it to be a disaster."

Romy and I followed Shannon inside. We found Daniel in a hallway and Shannon asked him if his offer still stood. "Yeah, sure," said Daniel. "Let me just finish this." He drank from his beer. Daniel had short blond hair and was wearing an oversized black t-shirt and a cross necklace. I looked at my phone and saw that the battery had died. "What time is it?" I thought. "Something something a.m.," I thought. About fifteen minutes later, Romy and I sat on the ground in Daniel's bathroom and drank beers while Shannon sat in the tub.

"There's just one rule," said Daniel, "and it's not even a rule, but I get to decide what I am giving you."

"Just do something," said Shannon. "I don't care." She laughed. Daniel activated the electric trimmer and began to shave the left side of Shannon's head. He was drinking but didn't look drunk, or maybe I was drunk enough to perceive him as sober. Daniel said, "Stand still," a few times. Shannon kept laughing and wondering aloud if this was a good idea and then laughing again. About fifteen minutes passed. Daniel turned off the trimmer and observed Shannon from multiple angles.

"There," said Daniel. "Work of art."

"I need to see this," said Shannon. She got up and rushed to the mirror and then stared at her reflection for a few seconds.

"Do you like it?" said Daniel.

"It's good," said Shannon. "It's hard to tell, I am a little drunk. I don't know if my brain knows what symmetry is anymore. I think I like it."

"Cool," said Daniel.

"Do you think you could do Thomas?" said Shannon.

"Yeah, let's keep going," said Daniel. "This is fun."

Daniel instructed me to come sit in the tub. As I was getting up, a girl opened the bathroom door without knocking and explained that she really needed to pee, but didn't mind doing that with us in the room if we all looked away. We all looked away. Later, Daniel shaved both sides of my head and then improvised a haircut using scissors for the rest. "Oh my god," said Shannon. She laughed. After he was done, I said, "Thank you," and then got up and looked at myself in the mirror. Observing my reflection, I felt less agony than the usual amount of agony. I had no idea if I liked or disliked the haircut, but didn't care. I said, "Thank you," again and Daniel said, "No problem." He then insisted that Romy let him cut her hair and managed to convince her by telling her that he would only shave the lower back of her head. She didn't seem confident, but sat in the bathtub and went through with it anyway.

About twenty minutes later, on the back porch, Shannon, Romy and I observed our respective haircuts. We all looked funnier and seemed more interesting to stare at. I was drunk and still had several beers in my backpack and didn't want to drink them, because the taste of alcohol was starting to feel redundant. I gave one to Romy and then two more to random people sitting next to us. I saw Shannon talking to someone else. A few minutes later, she inhaled white powder from the person's house key, opening a door to something. I went back inside, to the main area. Electronic music with no discernible rhythm or pattern was playing. Daniel was dancing aggressively and enthusiastically, encouraging other people to get into it. I danced cynically at first, but then got more into it as time went on, which was unexpected. "Coherent human being," I thought. "Young professional," I thought. The song went on and on, felt like hundreds of songs superimposed, colliding, yelling at one another. I wanted to finish the song, but then grew bored after about forty-five minutes.

Near the bathroom, I found Romy and mentioned that I was thinking of leaving and she replied, "Me too." We tracked down Daniel and said goodbye and then located Shannon and tried saying goodbye, but had to negotiate with her a little. "Why are you leaving? Don't go," said Shannon. "We're just going," I said. "We'll see you soon."

Exiting the building, I looked at the sky for a few seconds while Romy checked her phone. The moon looked like a rerun of old footage. I couldn't think of a way to get back home and so asked Romy if I could sleep on her couch. I didn't want her to think I was going to try anything if she didn't want me to, so I specified, "And by couch, I mean couch." I immediately regretted adding that. I thought, "Wait, why shouldn't I try anything?" I wanted to sleep with her. I wanted to sleep with her in her bed. I wanted to sleep with her in her bed, our bodies lying in odd positions next to one another, like a kind of self-conscious floral arrangement.

We walked to her apartment.

"I am stupid," I said.

"Why are you stupid?" said Romy.

"I don't know," I said. "Why did I drink so much?"

"It happens," said Romy. "I shouldn't have let him cut my hair. I wouldn't have let him if I hadn't been drunk. I didn't want to say anything, but I don't know if I like it."

"It looks fine," I said. "You look like a fashionista on coke. I look like there's a small duck resting on my head."

"We look like we could be on Shannon's Tumblr," said Romy.

"We should do a photo shoot," I said. "Sell expensive brands of jeans to people."

"Trade the jeans for weed," said Romy.

We turned left on a small street and then left again on another street and stopped in front of an old apartment building. I waited as Romy looked for her keys. We entered and removed our shoes. A cat greeted us.

"Catherine is probably asleep," said Romy. "Also, I guess I should warn you, he hates guys, so he might be an asshole to you."

"Your cat hates guys," I said.

"Any guy we've brought home, the cat was being really defensive about it," said Romy. "Maybe it's jealous."

"Is it your cat or Catherine's cat?" I said.

"It's both ours," said Romy. "A friend of ours was giving kittens away, so we took one. For now, we're pretending we own half a cat each, like I own the front half and she owns the butt half. We'll figure out who really owns it later. Probably Catherine."

We moved to the living room and then sat on the couch and talked at a low volume for a few minutes. I was tired and Romy seemed tired. I tried petting the cat, but it failed to react.

"Did you have pets as a kid?" I said.

"Not really," said Romy. "This is my first cat. I didn't think I would be a cat person, but I actually like it. I tell people about my cat sometimes. With pets, they don't care, they always give you the same amount of affection. It's nice. With people, you never know how much affection you're going to get. Some weeks you get a lot and then other weeks you sleep alone."

"Your cat is a robot cat," I said. "It doesn't respond to my petting."

"You just need to pet it harder," said Romy.

"I can hear all the gears inside," I said.

I thought Romy would laugh, but she didn't. There was a pause. I thought, "Maybe she wants me to make a move, kind of like when I kissed her coming out of Casa." I didn't want to make a move. I wanted her to desire me. I wanted her to desire me and look at her face and sense within the face a custom-made expression of desire. I kind of wanted to ask her, "What are your needs?" directly, just to see what would happen. So far, we hadn't expressed our needs or desires directly to one another, had only hinted at them indirectly, burying them through conversation. "Feels like we're always stalling in ambiguous territory," I thought. "This is bad. I don't understand how we're still at that stage. I can make a move, she might even go for it, but I really feel like it should come from her at this point. If it doesn't, this isn't going to work and I am probably just wasting my time."

I did nothing.

We said good night and she retreated to her room.

I lay down on the couch.

I texted Cristian for some reason.

I felt like my life was horrible, minus good living conditions.

I fell asleep.

In the morning, Romy's cat jumped on me. I was already awake, but trying to convince myself I wasn't. "Robot cat," I thought. "Trying to end the human race," I thought. My phone was still dead, but I guessed that it was about eleven a.m. I decided to let myself out discreetly.

Cutting through the park, I saw that people were playing with dogs, doing yoga poses, throwing Frisbees, sunbathing, resting.

"Why are people relaxing at a time like this? Shouldn't everyone feel concerned about their relationship with Romy?" I thought.

Later, at the metro station, I felt confident that I could overcome the turnstile.

"Do you remember what you texted me last night?" said Cristian. He laughed. "I saw it this morning. I thought it was really funny."

"I think I texted you something like, 'I am drunk,'" I said.

"Actually, it says, 'I am druna,'" said Cristian.

"Oh," I said.

"'I am druna,'" said Cristian. He laughed again. "Why were you trying to tell me you were drunk?"

"I think I just wanted to text something to someone," I said.

Hand on my shoulder. I turned around, saw Julian, made a face. "Thomas, could I see you in private?" said Julian. I replied, "Sure," and then grabbed my notebook and followed him to a small room. He closed the door behind me, sat on the chair opposite mine, observed me in silence for a few seconds. I observed him back. "Endurance," I thought. Around us were two silver chairs, a white round table, a black phone, a laminated poster featuring a giant Tetris block making a face while hurling itself at other blocks, carpet.

"So," said Julian. "This might be a delicate conversation."

"You probably wouldn't have called me here if it was good news," I said. "I am guessing it's something like, Scrabble is cancelled. Or being shipped off to Romania. Or we're getting merged with another project, like Plants vs. Zombies."

"Scrabble vs. Zombies," said Julian. "Genius! Write me a proposal right now!"

He laughed. I kept a straight face.

"No, that's not exactly it, though that would be an interesting proposition," said Julian. "The reason why I've asked you here is that I want to talk to you about your motivation level."

"What do you mean?" I said.

"Your attitude," said Julian. "You don't seem very happy or even interested these days. I've had a long discussion with Carl. He says he never sees you play the builds and that you usually come in late and look like you don't want to be here. He doesn't have a lot of faith in you anymore and, frankly, I think I agree with him. You don't seem very focused. The last few meetings, I didn't see you taking any notes, or hardly."

"Yeah, but," I said.

"I get it," said Julian. "You're tapped out. Scrabble isn't the most exciting project. You've been working on it for too long. I get that. But it's also a bit of a cash cow for the studio, so it needs to be right. We're going to switch you out and give you something easier, okay?"

"It doesn't sound like I have a choice," I said.

"I am informing you," said Julian, "but essentially, yes."

"I am a little disappointed," I said. I wasn't. I felt mostly unaffected by the news. "But if you feel that's for the best. And I guess you're right. I have been out of it lately."

"There you go," said Julian. "This is only a precautionary measure. Right now, as you know, we don't have a lot of new projects coming in, so I have resources that are in between titles, doing research and all kinds of things while I figure it out. I don't have a new project for you, but I've had a talk with Sebastian and he said he might need help, so you're going to assist him for now. We're going to move you to a new desk so that you're closer to him. Don't worry about Scrabble, someone else is going to take over. We might need you to help out with the transition."

"Sure," I said.

It suddenly dawned on me that writing weird poems felt like the closest thing to "play" I had experienced in years.

Entire lives archived on the internet like garbage piled up in a landfill.

Because Ines had signed up for e-bills, I had no idea how much money we owed the power company. I found an old bill with the account number on it and then set up a system with Cristian and Brent where I collected a fixed amount from everyone and then transferred that amount to the power company via online banking. My reasoning was that doing that each month would get our bill to go down, regardless of how much money we owed.

"Are you insane?" shouted Brent. "Are you completely drunk? Are you having a seizure, on coke?" Laura had said something and then changed her mind and then changed her mind again. "Congratulations on being the craziest person alive."

My new desk at work was located in a corner. I had a programmer neighbour and a wall neighbour and no one watching what I was doing.

For Cristian's birthday, Brent's gift was a case of Pabst Blue Ribbon wrapped in naked women from an adult magazine. "Beer wrapped in tits," said Cristian excitedly. My gift to him was a first-person shooter that I had purchased through work. In the video game, a soldier was able to operate a complicated, high-tech weapon with incredible speed and accuracy, but couldn't sit on a chair.

Internet porn didn't judge me.

"What is that, is that someone?" said Romy. It was the first week of August and we were walking back from the convenience store. I was carrying a bottle of wine from France. Judging from the label, the wine seemed convinced that it had been made in a castle. "It's not moving," I said. Getting closer, we realized that the silhouette belonged to a statue made of plastic. The statue had been abandoned on the sidewalk and was of a man with a handlebar moustache wearing a red, white and blue uniform. The head's upper third was missing.

"Are they getting rid of this?" said Romy.

"Why does it say 'Jack Daniels' on the back?" I said.

"I like how the proportions are all wrong," said Romy.

"It's what the God of body-image issues would look like," I said.

"We should keep it," said Romy. "Put it in your backyard. Make people pray to it."

" 'Dear God, please accept this sacrifice of a sweater with a bike on it,' " I said. "It doesn't look that heavy, we could probably carry it. Wait."

I tilted the statue to see if we could double-team it, realized that it was hollow inside, making it more cumbersome than heavy. I took the front end while Romy took the back end. Transporting the statue, I kept laughing and almost dropped the wine a few times, but then managed not to. At the house, we manoeuvred through the front door and then around the couch and kitchen table. We dropped the statue in the backyard, next to the shed, then took turns going to the bathroom to wash our hands. A few minutes later, I opened the bottle of wine and poured its content into two wine glasses and then stared at the label, which was written entirely in French. I felt relieved that I still understood what the words meant. "Just checking," I thought.

"I never drink wine," I said. "It's kind of funny to be drinking wine in these. We've been using them as normal glasses, so it feels wrong for some reason."

"I actually drank wine last night," said Romy. "I have this essay due tomorrow and I wanted to work on it, but then Catherine bought wine and we ended up drinking it and complaining about people we both like."

"How are your classes going?" I said.

"It's a train wreck so far, but summer classes are only six weeks long, so I'll be done soon," said Romy. "I keep handing things in late or half-finished. It's not even that much work. I just can't get myself to do anything. I have been really pathetic since I got back. The most productive thing I did today was drawing an elephant. I have no idea how people write books that are nine hundred pages long."

"Have you always had problems getting things done?" I said.

"This is a new low," said Romy. "It almost feels like a cry for help. I keep thinking it's only going to get worse."

"Not being in school anymore is hard," I said. "One thing school is good for is that it keeps feeding you little goals that feel meaningful to accomplish. It even grades you for them. When you stop school, you kind of expect work to fill that void, and it can do that to a degree, except it never gives you that same clear sense of progression. It's really easy to start feeling like you're stagnating and going nowhere."

"That's sort of how I feel," said Romy. "Stagnating. I've been Skyping with Lev. We've talked about me going to New York and staying with him for a while. He told me I wouldn't have to pay rent if I stayed with him, so I can sublet my room here. I think that's what I'll do after I am done with school. I can't be at home because it's too depressing and I can't seem to motivate myself to do anything here, so I might as well go over there."

"Do you really think it'll work out?" I said.

"Maybe not, but it seems better than doing nothing," said Romy.

"So you started talking to Lev again," I said.

"We've never really stopped," said Romy. "Not officially."

"Is that why you've been acting cautious around me?" I said.

"What do you mean?" said Romy.

"I kind of like you and wanted to get closer to you," I said, "and after the hospital thing, it felt like that was going to happen, but then I kept waiting for you to react to what was going on and it was like you were trying to suppress it instead of acknowledging it."

"I can see why you saw it that way," said Romy. "I mean, I wasn't trying to lead you on or anything. It's just, getting drunk, not thinking things through, that's kind of what I do."

She laughed nervously.

"Why do you have such a fascination with him?" I said. "Lev. He was an asshole to you."

"It's complicated," said Romy. "Lev is interesting. He has this philosophy where he says he doesn't experience suffering."

"That's bullshit," I said.

"It sounds like bullshit," said Romy, "but in practice it just makes him fun to be around. He doesn't bother with could-haves, would-haves or should-haves and has this capacity to accept whatever situation he's in. He's also really good at finding loopholes that allow him to do whatever he wants all the time and get away with it."

"That's the stupidest thing," I said. "Pretending you're not suffering is not not suffering. It's denial."

"I know the not suffering thing is weird," said Romy, "but it's hard to talk about that with him. He has this aura where you don't want to argue with him too much and just go with it."

"That's probably what makes him an asshole in the first place," I said. "Plus, I love my sorrows."

I said, "I love my sorrows" a second time in my head and it felt good.

"This scared the shit out of me," said Laura about the statue. "I went to pee at two a.m. and thought there was someone standing around in the backyard."

"Can we make one of those pacts where if we're both not married by the time we're forty, we kill everyone?" typed Shannon on Facebook Chat.

"I borrowed money from my mom," said Cristian. He still hadn't found a job or even looked for one. "She keeps telling me that I can move back in anytime I want. I don't know if I could. Maybe if it was the other way around, like she moves in with me. My rules now, asshole."

I stared at my work computer. Sebastian didn't really need me to assist him, only gave me little tasks from time to time, almost out of pity. Overall, it felt as if my job title had been changed to "Ghost," since no one in the studio talked to me or acknowledged me or asked me for anything anymore. I thought about the studio being downsized in the near future and my immediate superiors disliking me and my position now being redundant. "Good job," I thought. I felt confident that I would be let go during the next round of layoffs, which would probably occur before the end of the year. In the meantime, I was paid to do nothing, didn't have any responsibilities, spent most of my days reading things on the internet, writing poems, submitting them to literary magazines. Whether I was present or absent seemed to make absolutely no difference. Deep down, I knew that this was exactly what I had wanted to happen. I felt like what I had tried to do, more or less consciously, was to use self-destruction as a form of self-medication, to put myself in a position that would force me to quit my job, abandon video games as a career, go back to school full-time. I viewed transforming my life not as a drastic, impulsive move, but as a careful and methodical operation, like turning a boat around or, in this case, sinking it.

Name a time of the day and I have eaten cereal at it.

On Facebook, a status update from Romy informed me that she had completed her degree with lacklustre grades and was now looking for a rideshare to New York.

I thought, "I don't want to make an effort, that sounds like so much effort."

We still hadn't paid our rent for the month, but Brent and Cristian didn't seem too stressed about it. It was the third week of August. As usual, I assumed that we would wait for Pierre to pressure us for rent money before reacting.

Chatting on Facebook with Shannon from my work computer, I told her that I was free and then left early in the afternoon, during my lunch break, to go hang out with her. I didn't go back, knowing that no one at the studio would notice or care that I was gone. "What else can I get away with?" I thought.

My brain was my bedroom, my bedroom was just a thing.

I wanted to deconstruct my regrets in a way that proved they were made from a million tiny disappointments.

After placing the tigers on opposite walls, as if staging a dramatic face-off, Cristian observed the photographs from the point of view of someone entering the house, seemed satisfied with himself. He had brought back home two laminated photographs that someone down the street had attempted to throw out. The first photograph featured a tiger running in tall grass, while the second featured an annoyed tiger looking directly at the camera lens. It was the last Friday of August and about two hours before the final Cinedrome of the year, something that Brent had decided without discussing it with anyone and that I had been informed of by our Facebook event. Brent had later mentioned that he was starting a "medical film training project" soon and would have to concentrate on it full-time.

As Cristian was looking for our broom, a man in maybe his mid-thirties, wearing jeans, a gray jacket and sunglasses, opened the front door without knocking and then let himself in.

"Do you live here?" said the man abruptly, in English but with a heavy French accent.

"We do," I said. "Are you here for the screening? You're a little early."

"We know what you're doing," said the man.

"What do you mean?" I said.

"What you're doing is illegal," said the man. He reached for his left pocket and then quickly flashed what appeared to be a badge. I made a face. The man was apparently a police officer, though for some reason wasn't wearing a uniform. "We're getting reports that you've been using this space as a public venue. This is a residential area. We've received complaints from your neighbours about the noise level, and there might be other issues as well."

"We've used the backyard to screen movies for our friends in the past, but we've always tried to be respectful and make sure we end before eleven," I said. "Nothing else is happening here. That's all."

"That's all that's happening?" said the man.

"Yes," I said.

"If you want to organize events, please, rent a proper venue," said the man. "We'll have this address on our list from now on. The next step after this could be a fine. Have a good night."

As the man let himself out, I thought, "Shit."

"Who was that?" said Brent, coming out of his room.

"A cop," I said. "I think."

"What do you mean, 'I think?'" said Brent. "What did he say?"

"He wasn't wearing a uniform," said Cristian. "He showed us a badge, but it looked fake. Like it could have been something he bought at a dollar store."

"He said they knew what we were doing with the screenings and everything," I said. "He wanted us to stop. He said they might fine us."

"Shit," said Brent. "So it was a cop?"

"I don't know," said Cristian. "It could be a crazy neighbour who hates us, pretending he's a cop to try and get us to stop doing the screenings."

"Would you do that?" said Brent. "Can you imagine yourself walking into a random stranger's house and pretending you're a cop? That's insane. No one would do that."

"I would," said Cristian.

"Yeah, well, whatever," said Brent. "If he was a cop or not, it doesn't matter. We're done after tonight anyway, so it won't be a problem."

"We could still cancel the screening tonight," I said.

"Fuck it," said Brent. "I'd rather go for it. Nothing will happen."

"Are you sure?" I said.

Brent said, "Yeah, yeah," and then glanced back at his computer and became distracted by information onscreen. Cristian and I finished cleaning the house. About half an hour later, guests began to arrive. From a distance, I saw Romy coming in. She was wearing black pants and a pale teal t-shirt with a realistic-looking goose on it. I went to say hi. We hugged briefly and then retreated to my room, sat on the bed.

"I am leaving tomorrow morning," said Romy. "I still have to pack. I wanted to come say goodbye."

"I am happy you did," I said. "How are you? Are you nervous about heading there?"

"Not really," said Romy. "It's like I am indifferent to it. I feel like I am trading a nowhere for another nowhere."

"How are you getting to New York?" I said.

"I booked a rideshare from Craigslist," said Romy. "I am pretty sure it's one of those sketchy semi-organized vans."

"I love the vans," I said.

"Really?" said Romy. "I hate the vans."

"I am probably the only one who likes them," I said. "When I was growing up, my parents were stressed about money. For some reason, they owned this dark purple van. It's strange to imagine them driving around in it, because it seems so out of character now. The van rideshares remind me of that period, the van period. They make me think of terrible road trips to go visit my mom's family, with my mom being anxious because we're running late, my dad being angry at other drivers and calling them maniacs, and my sister and me sitting in the back seat trying to exist as little as possible, because we didn't want to get yelled at."

"You like the vans because they're terrible?" said Romy.

"Kind of," I said.

"I hadn't seen it that way," said Romy. "The vans always make me feel like I am being smuggled into a country."

She laughed nervously.

"Did you find someone to sublet your room?" I said.

"Yeah, that's taken care of," said Romy. "It's this girl Catherine knows. She's a bit of an airhead. She keeps talking to me about cosmetics and different kinds of spas and how she finds her therapist attractive. She'll be perfect."

"I should hit on her," I said. "Ask her to the prom."

"You're probably too late for that," said Romy, "unless you guys are planning a special backyard prom."

"Backyard prom," I said. "That would be really funny."

"So tonight is the last screening," said Romy.

"It is," I said. "I am going to miss having people over every Friday. Fall semester is starting soon, though. Maybe I'll get distracted and won't think about it too much."

"What classes are you taking?" said Romy.

"I have to decide soon," I said. "I am still registered part-time, so I have to choose whether I want to go full-time or not. I can sign up after classes have started, but the more I wait, the worse it'll get. The maximum I can wait is three weeks, I think."

From outside, I heard Brent shouting something and then laughing. Romy mentioned having to go and then we both stood up and hugged goodbye. While hugging, I focused on one of the jellyfish in the common area, which was dangling from its string and about to fall. I wasn't sure what I felt, maybe nothing, maybe the beginning of a delayed reaction, a slow bleed, the way sea turtles experience pain. A few minutes later, I sat next to Cristian and helped him with the bar. I heard Brent asking Cristian if we had lighter fluid and Cristian said, "I think so, in one of the pantries."

The movie we were screening was *Pink Flamingos*. The film drew a strong reaction from the crowd, a mix of applause and laughter and some yelling at events occurring onscreen. I looked around a few times. "No sign of cops," I thought. "Weed," I thought. After the movie, the audience clapped loudly. Brent, holding a bottle of lighter fluid, stood in front of the screen.

"Thank you for coming, everyone," said Brent. "This was our last screening of the year. If you have spare change or bills, I encourage you to donate. You saw a movie for free tonight, you all had a good time, anything you have helps us. Now, since our screen probably won't make it through another winter, I thought that tonight, as a special treat, I would put on some Vivaldi and set the frame on fire for your enjoyment."

The audience cheered. Brent moved over to the sound system and put on *The Four Seasons* and then began spraying lighter fluid on the screen. "Go for it!" someone yelled. Brent said, "Okay, okay," and then lit a match, but the resulting flames died quickly, doing little to no damage. Cristian went over to help. He sprayed more fluid, but couldn't get a fire going either. Someone in the front row shouted advice. Brent tried again. This time, flames appeared, moved from the inside to the outside, tearing through the screen's fabric. "Yes!" shouted Brent, raising his arms in victory. The flames began attacking the wooden structure. Several pictures were taken. Brent and Cristian observed the fire from up close for several minutes, smiling, looking emotional a little and genuinely happy.

Jackhammers. "We can't have screenings in the backyard, but they can do insanely loud construction at nine in the morning, no problem!" I heard Brent yell.

I suddenly realized that Pierre hadn't collected or even asked us for August's rent. I mentioned this to Cristian, who simply replied, "Maybe he died," while shrugging his shoulders.

The first week of September, I skipped work on Monday and then told myself I would go in on Tuesday, but then thought, "What's the point?" and at night went out with Cristian and Kyle again and skipped Tuesday as well. In this manner, I ended up not going to work for four consecutive days, with no one contacting me about my absences. I awoke on Friday morning around eleven a.m. and thought about heading to the office, but then started thinking about how little of me there was left there. "Almost nothing," I thought. I came to realize that I had two options. The first option was to go to work and officially resign. The second option was to continue not showing up until someone became aware that I was doing this. "How long would it take them to notice?" I thought. I imagined different units of time, a week for them to notice, two weeks, a month, like a high score from an arcade machine.

About half an hour later, I biked to work. I went in and saw that Julian wasn't sitting at his desk and then deduced that he was probably stuck in a meeting somewhere. "Perfect," I thought. I walked to my work computer, entered my password, began composing an email addressed to him. "Hi," read the email. "This week will be my last week. I am officially resigning. If you need anything from me to confirm my departure or if you need to reach me next week or beyond, the home address you have on file is still correct. Best of luck in the future." I pressed the Send button, grabbed personal belongings from my desk, placed them in my backpack, left without saying goodbye to anyone.

I signed up for several classes, the earliest of which was at one p.m. My plan was to survive using the money I had saved in my bank account and then apply for student loans after that. "Full-time," said my student account.

By text message, Brent asked me to log into his computer and retrieve information saved on his computer desktop. He had begun pre-production on the medical film training project, though wouldn't be filming until late October. Brent was hoping to purchase a new camera by combining the money he would be making for this contract with the money we had made over the summer with Cinedrome. The password to his computer was "Hugeballs," one word.

Rice.

The receptionist at the hair salon greeted me in English and then we talked for a full minute before she asked me for my name. I said, "Thomas," using the French pronunciation and she made a face and then we switched to French.

"It'll be great, we'll sell hot cocoa and everything," said Cristian to Shannon. The three of us were drinking beers in the park, sitting in the soccer nets as if they were hammocks. "That sounds great," said Shannon. Cristian had been telling people that he was going to build an ice rink in our backyard during the winter. He liked their reaction to that announcement, which made him feel as if he had a purpose in life, was doing something with himself.

"I told you, I am the get laid fairy," said Shannon. We were at a bar at two a.m. and she was looking around, trying again to find me someone to hook up with. "I get everyone laid. It's easy. You just get the girl drunk and talk about orgasms. You can use that trick on random chicks from now on."

After a few years of working in office-like environments, I suddenly didn't have a reason to get up in the morning anymore. My internal body clock had reset itself back to its default setting, letting me stay up until whenever, waking me not because I had obligations, but because I felt rested. This, at first, had felt a little like experiencing jet lag, but in the context of real life, a kind of life lag.

"How did I ever get up in the morning?" I typed to Shannon on Facebook Chat. "I used to be really good at it. But also, I hated my life."

"Hi," typed Shannon, along with an emoticon. We were in a new class together and the class involved sharing and discussing short stories we had written, instead of poems. "I just realized that we need to read Judith's story for tomorrow. I thought about doing it, but now it's four p.m. and I feel tired and drained and don't even want to look at it because my degree is useless and get me drunk tonight."

"Can we?" I typed. "Get drunk, I mean."

"I don't know," typed Shannon. "I feel very attached to these pink sweatpants right now."

"I haven't looked at Judith's thing either," I typed. "I kind of want to not read it and just go in and comment generic things at random during class instead. Like, 'In your piece, there's a tension between your tension and the other tension.'"

"I just feel so awkward when we have to talk about her work," typed Shannon. "She's so bland. I can't believe she's an actual person. I feel like we should critique her instead of her submission."

"Most people would enjoy that, I think," I typed. "It would be democratic."

"I wish that was a class," typed Shannon. "Personal critiques, sort of like group therapy. It would boost my GPA."

"There's a tension between your personality and our willingness to take you seriously," I typed.

"By the way, how do I ask for an extension in my other class?" typed Shannon. "I have no excuse."

"Would the extension really help, though," I typed, "or would it just delay you being fucked?"

"Obviously delay," typed Shannon.

"That seems bad," I typed. "We should set up a system where everyone's decisions are made by a third party who's one step removed. Like my roommate Cristian decides that you don't ask for an extension, Judith makes my personal decisions for me, etc."

"Or maybe some kind of decision raffle," typed Shannon.

"I wish," I typed.

Hometown dream: I dreamt that I moved back into my parents' house, but couldn't speak French anymore, could only express myself in English and hope other people understood me.

Fall. Rakes screaming, more leaves on the ground than trees in sight.

" 'Litost' is a word in Czech that means a moment in life where you realize that your life has taken on a tragic dimension," read my short email to Shannon. It was the third week of September. I was emailing her from class, simply transcribing a sentence the teacher had said.

I received an email from Romy, though not the kind I had anticipated. Instead, the email was a forward to me of a request from the Concordia bookstore. The bookstore was planning a reading around mid-October to showcase zines and chapbooks curated by students or alumni of the creative writing program. In the forwarded email, the person in charge of the bookstore was asking Romy if she knew anyone from her zine who would be available to perform a reading, and this was Romy's way of recommending me.

Coming back from school, I saw that Cristian and Brent had started a "landlord death pool" on the fridge. We still hadn't heard from Pierre, who hadn't contacted us or asked us for rent in almost two months. Cristian had bet that Pierre had suffered a heart attack while Brent had bet that Pierre had fallen down a flight of stairs, was still in the hospital and not actually dead.

I took my laptop to a computer store for repairs and was told that the process would take about five days. It was the first week of October. I had fallen asleep with the laptop next to me in the bed, knocking it on the floor in my sleep and damaging the screen. Later, to get work done, I used the public workstations at the Concordia University library. I logged into the system, was greeted by a cartoon wizard, who twirled on himself and then disappeared.

"It's fine," said Cristian. He was placing cigarettes in the microwave. "I have done this before. I only put them in for a few seconds. It makes them crisper, but that's it. Cigarettes are expensive and I don't have enough money to buy a new pack. I only spilled Sprite on these. They're still good."

My Facebook profile carrying on for me after my death, making new friends, wishing them happy birthday, attending events, staying relevant within various social circles.

I was still collecting a fixed amount from Brent, Cristian and myself once a month and then, via online banking, transferring the money to the power company to pay back our bill. Or at least trying to, as Cristian was often late in making regular payments. I didn't want to be the responsible one, wanted to be Cristian's friend more than I wanted to be mean to him or pressure him, and so didn't. As an authority figure, I was like the cartoon wizard, easily dismissed.

After shaving, I observed my face as if looking for another face within the face.

At a house party, Cristian told a girl that he was planning on constructing an ice rink from scratch in our backyard during the winter, expecting her to be impressed by this. The girl mentioned that her dad used to build ice rinks when she was little and started asking Cristian questions like, "Do you have a second water hose," wanting to know more details about how exactly he was planning to do this. Then Cristian seemed to realize, mid-conversation, that he had no idea how to actually build an ice rink.

My reading at the Concordia bookstore for Romy's zine went average. I talked too much before the reading began and had no saliva left by the time it was my turn to read, making it more difficult for me to pronounce certain words in English. I also discovered, while performing, that some of my poems were too long and contained awkward lines about death that for some reason had seemed okay on the page, but then were embarrassing when read aloud to a crowd by me.

I awoke and checked my phone for the time and then tried sleeping again, but could no longer find sleep at the place where I had left it, could only find some sort of failed lying around. It was ten a.m. and a Friday and the third week of October. I heard someone knocking on the front door, Brent answering and then a person mumbling in French. Brent explained to the person that he didn't speak French. The person mumbled something in English and Brent said, "Hold on," and then banged on my door. "Thomas, you need to talk to the guy that's here," said Brent, sounding concerned. I made a face. I got up and put on a black sweater with thin blue lines intersecting. Coming out of my room, I saw a man wearing a navy blue jumpsuit opening the electricity panel in the kitchen.

"What's happening?" I said to the man in French.

"We have to cut your electricity," said the man. "I am very sorry. Your account is currently billed for more than $2,100. You have payments coming in, but they're infrequent. We sent several disconnection notices. It didn't seem like you would be paying."

"We didn't receive them," I said. "Wait, can we send money now?"

"I can't wait for them to confirm the payment," said the man. "You'll have to call the number that's on the flyer right there and deal with them. You'll have to pay the full amount to get your power back. I am very sorry. I have to cut you off."

"Wait," I said.

The man pulled a switch. Lights in all rooms went out and the house stopped making sounds. The man closed the panel, repeated that he was sorry, left.

"Did we just lose our power for real?" said Brent.

"They thought we wouldn't be paying them the full bill, so they cut us off," I said.

"How much do we owe?" said Brent.

"He said we owe $2,100," I said. "Some of this might be because of Dan, I don't know how much. I thought if we sent them money every month it would lower our bill over time and get them to leave us alone, but it didn't."

"How is it even possible that we owe this much?" said Brent. "That's insane."

"Hi," said Cristian, coming out of his room, looking half-awake. "Why the noise? And why is the power out?"

"We just got cut off," said Brent.

"He said we would have to pay the entire thing if we want our power back," I said. "$2,100."

"I don't have that money," said Cristian. "I don't have money."

"Let's just call them and see what they say," I said. "Maybe we can work out a deal."

"You do that," said Brent. "I have to go. You guys take care of it. I'll be back tonight. Stupid shit."

Brent grabbed his camera and backpack from his room, ran out the door. I called the number on the power company's flyer and was placed on hold and the hold music sounded like a saxophone freaking out. I felt angry at the power company for cutting our power and also for forcing me to talk to them on the phone. I hated talking on the phone. A few minutes later, I was transferred to someone. I explained our situation and was told they could only speak to the account holder, which was Ines and not me. I hung up.

"Shit," I said. "They can't talk to me, they need to talk to Ines."

"I can call her," said Cristian. "I can get her to come by."

"That would be helpful," I said. "Thank you."

While Cristian was contacting Ines, I went to the grocery store and bought a yogurt packaged with cereal in a separate container and came back. I sat at the kitchen table and ate the yogurt and then wasn't sure what to do.

About half an hour later, Ines arrived at the house with Matthew.

"Looks like you guys have a bit of situation," said Ines. She examined the power company's flyer. "So why is my name still on this?"

"We never changed it," I said.

"They sent you the thing," said Ines. "The thing that says you were taking over the bill. You were supposed to sign it and send it back to them."

"Did I agree to that?" I said.

"Yes, you did," said Ines.

"I don't remember you telling me that," I said. "I don't remember agreeing to that."

"Well, fuck," said Ines.

I tried to recap what had happened, which failed to improve the situation. I stopped saying things. Ines agreed to contact the power company and went to another room to make the call. While waiting, Matthew tried making small talk with Cristian and me, but then we quickly reverted to silence.

"Okay," said Ines. "They said there's no other possible arrangement. We have to pay the entire amount to get the power back."

"Shit," I said.

"What do we do?" said Cristian.

"I don't know, but we have to clear that amount," said Ines. "I don't have that money and I don't want that amount in my name."

"It's not enough," said Cristian, "but we could use the money we made with Cinedrome. That would suck for Brent, though. He really wanted that camera."

"I can pitch in," said Ines. "I just can't be responsible for the entire amount."

"I'll have to pay for it," I said. "I mean, realistically, I don't see any other solution. We can't not have power and I am the only one whose bank account can take the hit. If you give me the Cinedrome money and Ines pitches in and you and Brent figure something out to give me back money, it wouldn't be so bad. We would all be paying a fair share."

"Yeah," said Cristian. "I mean, that could work."

"You have to give me back that money, though," I said. "I am serious. I need to avoid going on loans for as long as possible."

"I can probably borrow from my mom again," said Cristian, "or I can look for a job. Brent should be able to pay you back."

"Do you mind if I borrow your iPhone?" I said to Ines.

"Not at all," said Ines. "Here."

I used Ines' phone to access my online banking. I located the correct menu item, tapped on it, waited for the new page to load. I tapped on an item onscreen and entered the account number and then indicated that I wanted to transfer slightly more than $2,100 to it. I pressed the Confirm button. I looked at the amount remaining in my bank account and felt nauseous a little. Ines called the power company again and was told that it might take a few days for the payment to clear and that we needed to check back with them on Monday.

"Shit," I said.

"Early next week," said Ines. "That's not so bad. You just need to survive the weekend." I asked Cristian if he could stay with his mom for the next few days and he replied that he would think about it. "Brent can stay with us," said Ines. "Good," I said. I thanked Ines and Matthew for coming by and went back to my room. I changed clothes, grabbed my laptop and backpack, put on shoes. I left the house and headed to Concordia, didn't have classes that day, just needed to be somewhere that had heat and a Wi-Fi connection.

Over Facebook, I asked Shannon if I could stay at her apartment until our power situation was resolved. "Yes," typed back Shannon. "I am not going out tonight. Come! You can stay in the small room." A few hours later, in the evening, I went back home to grab personal items. The house was now cold, dark, hostile. I used the light emitted by the screen on my phone to find my way around the common area. I packed extra clothes and other belongings from my room. In the bathroom, I found one of Brent's dollar store flashlights on a shelf. I thought there might be hot water left in the water tank and then for some reason tried showering in the dark and the shower mercilessly attacked me with cold water. "Wow, that was a terrible idea," I thought, while putting on clothes again, shivering.

The next morning, Saturday, I awoke in the small room at Shannon's. I checked Facebook and saw that I had received a message from Mathieu, who I had been to high school with. I hadn't talked to Mathieu in years. From what I could tell from his profile picture, Mathieu had a stable life and was now a dad. He looked like a dad. It felt like a different amount of time had passed in my life than in Mathieu's life. I began composing a response and tried to explain what my life was like now, but then kept feeling like my sentences in French didn't sound quite right. Later, I gave up and didn't respond.

Best way to describe my relationship with my hair would be "Hostage situation."

The party we went to was hot and sweaty and felt like an incubator for casual sex.

On Monday morning, I called the power company to see if our payment had cleared. It hadn't. I called again a few hours later and then periodically throughout the day. "I hate life, I hate the power company, the power company is my life, I hate it," I thought. Around five p.m., I was told that the payment had been processed and that a technician would be coming by to restore our power on Tuesday, between seven a.m. and eight-thirty p.m. The employee I spoke to mentioned that the technician would need access to our electric panel, which was inside the house, and that we would have to make sure that someone was home to let him in. I texted Cristian to inform him of the situation. I asked if he could guard the house from seven a.m. until I got back from class, which would be around three p.m. Cristian texted back, "No problem." A few minutes later, I received a second text from him explaining that he had been sleeping at the house even though there was no power, because he still preferred that to staying with his mom.

In the backroom of a dimly lit bar, I sat at a long oak table next to Shannon and two of her friends. The music was too loud for conversation, so I sipped on a pint and observed the small stage. The band playing had recently been labelled a "rising act" by an influential blog and played pop songs about shadows or love as something you can have control over. It seemed sad how the band had worked so hard to get a large audience to pay attention to them, but didn't have anything in particular to communicate to that audience, only songwriting clichés. "Ironic," I thought, without being certain that this qualified as irony.

Returning from class on Tuesday, I passed by the house and saw that a note was duct-taped to the front door. "We were here at one-twenty p.m. No answer. Please call the following number to make another appointment," said the note from the power company. "Shit," I thought. The front door was locked. I went in and looked around and saw that no one was home. "Why isn't Cristian here?" I thought. "He was supposed to be here." I entered the house and sat in the common area and then called the number on the note. I made a new appointment for Wednesday. I tried reaching Cristian, but was redirected to his voicemail. I left a message and then texted him and left a third message for him on the kitchen table.

Lying on her bed, Shannon and I watched *Eternal Sunshine of the Spotless Mind* on her laptop. In the movie, an emotionally withdrawn man and his ex-girlfriend undergo invasive brain procedures in order to stop having to awkwardly acknowledge each other in public. "It's my parents' wedding anniversary next week," said Shannon. "Twenty-five years. I think they're expecting me to buy them a gift. This is so annoying. I have no idea what to get them. Why can't I just buy them drugs? Why can't drugs be the appropriate gift in all situations?"

"Hello," my voice said. I had awoken in the small room at Shannon's and let the first call go to voicemail, but then answered the second call. It was Wednesday, a little after nine a.m.

"Where are you?" asked Cristian.

"I am at Shannon's," I said. "Where are you?"

"At the house," said Cristian. "Why are you at Shannon's? You need to be here, I can't wait here all day. I have been doing job interviews. Well, I did one. I have another one this afternoon."

"You didn't tell me you were doing job interviews," I said.

"I need money," said Cristian.

"We missed the power guy yesterday," I said. "Why weren't you at the house?"

"I was," said Cristian. "Then you weren't coming back and I had an interview."

"I came back at three, like I said I would," I said. "Why didn't you contact me?"

"You didn't say three," said Cristian.

"I did," I said.

"Okay," said Cristian. "Well, we really need to get the power back. It's cold here. I dreamt of ice fishing last night."

"I'll be at the house in an hour," I said. "I won't go to my classes today, I'll just sit at home and wait for the power guy. Can you give me an hour?"

"I think so," said Cristian.

"Just hold on," I said. "I'll be there soon."

I hung up and walked to the bathroom. I locked the bathroom door, undressed, turned on both water taps, stepped in the shower. I felt angry in the shower, like I wanted to scream at the shower and maybe punch the shower, make threats to the shower. Later, I got out. In the small room, I changed clothes, grabbed my backpack, put on shoes. I exited Shannon's apartment and then walked down from Bernard, using alleys and side streets. Around Laurier, my phone rang again. As I reached for it, I thought, "I have been using my phone as a phone way too much lately."

I answered.

"Why aren't you at the house?" said Brent in an aggressive tone.

"I am on my way now," I said.

"How come we still don't have power?" said Brent. "It's insane. It's been five days. You need to go there now and harass them by phone and you wait there until the fucking technician puts our fucking power back on. Cristian needs to get himself a job. He shouldn't be dealing with that shit. It should be you."

"Look, we missed the power guy yesterday," I said.

"This isn't we, this is you," said Brent. "It's your responsibility. This is ridiculous. If you can't be there, you need to organize things. You talk to people and you organize things."

"How is this my responsibility?" I said. "It's not my responsibility, it's our responsibility."

"You need to get shit done," said Brent.

"Are you seriously yelling for real?" I said. "You're not even fucking there doing any fucking thing to help. Look, Cristian left the house yesterday before I got there and that's when the guy came. I am going there right now and I'll just sit there until it's settled. Now if you don't have anything constructive to add, you just shut the fuck up and go back to thinking you're better than whatever it is you're doing right now."

I think we were both surprised that I was yelling back.

I sent a text message to Brent and Cristian to inform them that our power had been restored. A few minutes later, Brent texted back, "Cool, thank you." I cleaned the fridge, which was in a rough state, and then the common area. Turning various lights on and off around the house felt pleasurable.

"I don't want bad blood with you," said Brent. "I was angry because I needed to upload insanely large files for the medical training stuff. I tried uploading them at Matthew's, but his internet kept timing me out. I tried at a café and it did the same thing. I have never had problems uploading stuff at the house. The client lost patience and told me I didn't have my shit together. I am pretty sure I lost that contract. That's why I was angry."

"You should have told me that," I said. "I might have been able to help. I think we were both annoyed because of the power situation and needed to yell and be angry. It happens. I am not angry anymore."

"Good," said Brent.

Skimming through our mail pile, I found the power company's disconnection notices.

I submitted revised poems to a reading series curated by one of my teachers at Concordia, most of which had been written at work.

Though we hadn't been in contact since she had moved to New York, Romy sent me two pictures taken with her phone. The first was a close-up of her face looking unimpressed, along with the caption "Underwhelmed," and the second was a picture of her right boob, along with the caption "My boob at a bad angle (I swear)." I made a face while staring at the boob.

The person waiting in line in front of me at the pharmacy was talking on his phone, in English but with a French accent. At one point, he couldn't think of a specific word, but made up for it by using the French equivalent, "moissisure," instead. Overhearing his conversation, I thought, "Moissisure." Then I thought, "Wait, what's 'moissisure' in English again?" and couldn't remember the word "mould" for some reason. The word "moissisure" taunted me in my head a little, as the only French word in an otherwise completely

English sentence. Examining the sentence, I no longer felt like my brain was set to either one language or the other. Instead, I felt like my brain was trapped in a neutral space between both languages.

Standing outside the front door of the house was a man with meticulously combed hair, wearing a blazer and a tie. After introducing himself as Lawrence, the man, a real estate agent, handed me a business card that featured his name, title, phone number, a company logo, as well as a picture of himself in which he was confident-looking and glowing. "Coherent human being," I thought. "Rape-free," I thought. The agent asked me if he could showcase the house as well as the backyard to prospective buyers and I replied, "Sure," even though I wasn't certain what this was about.

Facebook was my procrastination's thesis.

Lying to yourself is half the battle.

Halloween party at Kyle's house. I had drawn a little boat on my face and was wearing a sweater with nautical flags on it. People asked me about my costume and I explained it by saying, "I am a dreamboat," and then they laughed for a few seconds and that's how I survived the night.

I listened attentively to the voicemail message that Pierre had left on my phone.

"I've been meaning to come by," said Pierre to me in French. It was the first week of November. I offered Pierre water in a wine glass and then we sat around the kitchen table. The house was mostly silent. Pierre was still breathing heavily, and the noise coming from him was blending in nicely with the sound of wind blowing loudly against the kitchen window, some sort of spontaneous duet. "Relaxing," I thought. Pierre explained that the last two months had been difficult for him and that he had had health complications, but that he was better now. Because of this, he hadn't been able to collect rent from us for August, September and October, but that he would like to do so now. I replied that I could get him our rent for this month easily, but that everyone living here was on a limited income and so that we would need a little more time for the rest. "That's understandable," said Pierre. "I can give you time. But I'd like to settle this as soon as possible. Because of my health, I am making some changes in my life. I am looking at selling this building. I already have a potential buyer."

My email inbox contained two emails. The first email was a medium-sized email from Romy that contained multiple dramatic statements and mentioned that she was moving back to Montreal. "I miss you," the email said. The email missed me. I could tell the email meant it. The second email was from the reading series I had submitted poems to. The email wanted me to perform at the reading series' next event, on the last Wednesday of November.

"He can't just come back out of nowhere and expect us to pay him three months of rent all at once," said Brent.

"It's worse than that," I said. "We're in November now, so if you add November, that's four. He seemed understanding, like he would be willing to negotiate and meet us halfway, but if we don't do anything, technically, he could evict us."

"I'll be paid for the hours I did on the medical thing, but I have nowhere near that money," said Brent.

"I can't borrow anymore from my mom," said Cristian. "I tried."

"We could try paying him, like, a rent and a half every month until we pay him back," said Brent.

"But if he sells the building, then that would get really compli-cated," I said. "What we need as soon as possible is November's rent. The rest, I don't know."

"Right," said Brent. "Let's start with that. The eviction thing, if we pay November and figure out a way to get him maybe another month of rent on top of that, I don't think he would have grounds for eviction anymore. We would just owe him money. Maybe we can get away with it."

"The other thing," I said, "is that I bailed the house out of the money hole for the electricity bill, and I get that everyone's broke and that we're kind of fucked right now, but you guys need to do something about paying me back. I know this makes it worse, but I don't think I should be paying my share of the rent for November. I think you guys should pay it for me, as a way of paying me back for the money hole."

I wanted to contact Ines to inform her of the rent situation, but because of the electricity bill incident, I pictured myself telling her something like, "Sorry, I have more bad news," and couldn't even get through the imaginary situation without wanting to evaporate into a fine mist.

Brent gave me his share of November's rent and later Cristian contributed his share. Since Ines had signed post-dated cheques, the only share missing was mine. I had told Brent and Cristian that I was expecting them to pay for me and didn't want to budge on this, and so decided to give them more time to come up with the remaining amount.

My mom left a voicemail on my phone that I quickly deleted.

All I had to do to make the bus appear was to yell at it in my head.

"How will I check the internet when I am dead?" I thought.

"Are you Thomas?" said a man wearing a black jacket and leather gloves. "I was told to ask for you," he added. I confirmed I was. The man introduced himself as Amir and then shook my hand while exaggerating a smile.

"The transaction is still underway," said Amir, "so it might take a few more weeks for it to be official, but for all intents and purposes, I will be taking over from Pierre and acting as owner and landlord of this building from now on. I would like to perform some renovations during the winter."

"Do you have anything specific in mind?" I said.

"The basement below the building," said Amir. He paused. "The Rave Cave," I thought. "It's not in very good shape. In fact, on this floor, you're probably losing a lot of heat right now. I would start with that."

"Well, let us know what your plans are," I said. "I can leave you my number, if there's anything. Hold on."

"Actually, this is what I came here to talk to you about," said Amir. "I would be interested in repossessing the building for personal use. I would be renting these units to family members. Now, I understand you have a lease and this would involve breaking it off, but I would like to discuss this possibility with you. I would be willing to compensate you in a reasonable way for moving out."

"So he's willing to erase the rent debt," said Brent.

"That's the arrangement we came up with," I said. "I told him everyone here was broke and that the best thing he could offer us, as compensation for moving out, was financial relief. The plan is, he erases the money we owe to Pierre and we don't even have to worry about paying any rent anymore, but in exchange we have to move out before the end of the year. We're also responsible for our own moving fees and tying up any loose ends."

"That's not a bad deal," said Brent.

"But that means we won't be doing Cinedrome next summer," said Cristian.

"New owner guy probably wouldn't let us do it anymore anyway," said Brent. "Or the cops. How did you get him to say yes to erasing the rent debt? If you had asked me for that, I would have told you to go fuck yourself. Two months of rent would have been a fair compensation."

"I thought he was going to haggle with me," I said, "so I asked for more and he said yes almost right away. He seemed like he really wanted us to move out. Maybe that's less money to him than it is to us."

"Sounds like we're saying yes to this deal," said Cristian.

"Realistically, I don't think we have much of a choice," said Brent. "Tell him we'll move out."

"I'll contact him," I said.

"I guess I won't be doing the ice rink," said Cristian.

"So, wait, we never paid November's rent," said Brent.

"I told you I wasn't paying my share," I said. "You guys gave me your shares, but you never came up with the rest."

"Well, that's not a problem anymore," said Brent. "So can you give us that money back?"

"I kind of feel like I should be keeping it," I said. "It should go to paying me back for the electricity bill."

"We already gave you Cinedrome's money, plus Ines gave you money for that," said Brent. "That's a lot. To be honest, I don't think we owe you more. The money hole for the electricity bill, I don't even know who owes what. I wasn't here until April."

"The money hole is the money hole," I said. "It would take, like, quantum physics to analyze it and break it down into something that makes sense. There's Dan, Niklas, Ines, us, maybe even people that lived here before me. Brittany. I don't know."

"Let's look at the bill," said Brent. "Let's break down who owes what."

"I don't even have one," I said. "I could ask Ines, but I honestly wouldn't know where to start. It goes back too far. I don't think it's realistic to think that we'll be able to figure out how much exactly each of us owes. Even if we did, you try asking Niklas for money."

"You're defeatist for not even trying," said Brent.

"Maybe so," I said.

"No, exactly so," said Brent.

"I shouldn't have to pay for the money hole," I said. "I paid enough money for this stupid house. The only leverage I have now is to be a dick to you guys and withhold the money you gave me for November's rent. If I give it back, I'll be stuck with the money hole and will end up paying for it."

"That's extremely audacious," said Brent.

"Well, what do you want me to do?" I said. "I don't think we're going to come up with a solution that makes everyone happy. I think it's going to suck a little bit for all of us."

We negotiated for an hour and eventually settled on a compromise we all agreed wasn't completely unfair. Then we spent the next few days avoiding each other, hiding in our rooms, working our way around each other, like traffic cones. By text message, I asked Shannon if I could move into the small room at her apartment permanently. She said, "Are you sure you want the small room?" and then added, "It's small."

"I am back in Montreal," read a Facebook message from Romy. "What are you doing this week?"

Though at first I felt calm exchanging messages with Romy, I noticed that in her interactions with me, she seemed more eager and receptive than before. I tried to visualize what seeing her would be like, but wasn't sure what to expect. "It feels like she's completely changed her mind," I thought. I considered the possibility of Romy being interested in me now and began to feel apprehensive a little, progressively experiencing what felt like a downward spiral of self-doubt.

It seemed so much easier to imagine a scenario in which Romy being interested in me led to me letting her down, or looking terrible in comparison to Lev, or exposing myself as flawed, or all those things at once.

I had emailed Greg about helping me move again and we had agreed on a time and a day. He showed up at the house twenty minutes early, a little before one p.m., explaining that he had been called for an audition later that afternoon. It was the third week of November. "You don't have that much stuff, we can still move you," said Greg, "but I am thinking we should speed this up. Tell you what. If we're done by two-thirty, I'll only charge you forty. How does that sound?" I wanted to save money, so I said yes. A few minutes later, we began running in and out of the house, rushing boxes, garbage bags, other items into Greg's minivan. Moving my bed, with Greg on one end and me on the other, both of us laughing, I thought about how having to move my belongings as fast as possible was making the process of moving less of a chore, and more of a game.

"I think he didn't expect me to say yes when he offered," said Romy. We were sitting in the small room at Shannon's, which was now my room. "When I got there, we tried getting back into it, but then we just ended up fighting a lot. After a while, I could feel it, he had lost interest. He was gone all the time, like he kind of stopped sleeping at his apartment. He basically left me alone until I decided that I was going to leave. I kept thinking, 'Wow, this is awful,' about everything while I was there. At Duane Reade. 'Wow, this is an awful pharmacy.' Staring at people in the park. 'Wow, this is an awful chess match.' I don't know what I was expecting."

"Maybe you needed closure," I said.

"Maybe," said Romy. "I still only half-understand the subway system there. It's confusing. It's like everything I hate about poetry."

"Yeah," I said. "All the colours and letters, and colours that somehow turn into letters. The last time I was there, I got lost a little. I took the wrong train and had to walk for a while to get to where I was going. You know when you're in unfamiliar surroundings and everything suddenly seems more ominous? It's like, 'These guys are playing with a dog, I wonder if they're going to assault me.'"

"Then nothing happens and you're kind of disappointed," said Romy.

"Or, like, the dog barks at you," I said.

"I am sorry I sent you the boob picture," said Romy. "I was just going crazy. I felt bad when you didn't respond."

"I don't know," I said. "I mean, I didn't know what to say."

"I let myself be interested in you for one day and that's what happens," said Romy. "I thought about being back in Montreal and actually getting my shit together instead of just pretending, and seeing you instead of just pretending, and then I sent you the boob picture and you didn't respond, so I made up scenarios in my head to explain why you hate me now. I am not the best at thought experiments. I think my point is mostly that I am insane."

"I don't hate you," I said.

"I just want to stop feeling weird," said Romy. "Maybe I should be single for a while. Maybe I should be a nun."

"Thinking about this makes me feel really fucked," I said. "I mean, I like you and there's chemistry there for me, for sure, but at the same time, I feel like we're both cynical and emotionally damaged people who expect the worst out of relationships, like we think relationships and natural disasters are the same thing. If we were to start seeing each other, I am afraid we would just mess things up and end up not talking, and I don't want that. I also feel like you might need time to process the last few months. I don't know if I am making sense, I am probably making a lot of confusing statements."

"No, you're making sense," said Romy. "I mean, I don't disagree with you. I am also afraid it could fuck things up. I can't tell if giving up now would be disappointing or kind of a relief. Or both."

"We're being too rational about this," I said. "I don't know if we should be talking about this calmly, in terms of positives and negatives. We're listing things in columns like left-brained people. It should probably be something more impulsive, like we can't help ourselves and that's why it's happening."

"You're probably right," said Romy. "I am sorry if I've been an asshole to you."

"You haven't," I said. "I am the asshole. I poisoned you by accident. I've also been lying to you a little."

"About what?" said Romy, making a face.

"It's not that bad," I said. "It's just, I am actually older than what I told you, but only by one year. I don't know why I started lying. I think I was panicking because of the being back in school thing, like all of a sudden people around me were all so much younger than me. How do you stop lying when you're so used to the lie that the lie feels more like the truth than the truth?"

"So you're one year older," said Romy.

"Yeah," I said.

"Well, that's not a huge lie," said Romy. "It's kind of a sad lie, even. I don't think that makes you an asshole. I mean, I am not sure why you felt the need to lie, but that probably makes more sense to you than it does to me."

"I know," I said. "I agree. It's a sad lie. It's more like, I am starting to feel like I can't tell the difference between lying to people and lying to myself anymore. That's why I am telling you. To stop."

I thought about the face I was making, and then about every face I had ever made.

Updated my Facebook status to, "Filled with regrets, invite me to parties."

"I have been trying to email Romy," I typed to Shannon on Facebook Chat. We still felt comfortable communicating through Facebook, even though our rooms were now within shouting distance. "But so far my day has been, like, trying to write the email, giving up, napping, trying again, giving up again, napping again. I didn't make that much progress, except it felt like each nap had its own purpose, like the seven stomachs of a cow."

"Have you talked to her since you guys had your little chat?" typed Shannon.

"Not really," I typed.

"So nothing new happened?" typed Shannon.

"Nothing concrete," I typed. "I've just been going insane wondering if I was right or wrong to convince her not to go for it. It feels like only a deranged person would have made that decision."

"Maybe," typed Shannon.

"I am kind of hoping emailing her will remove the insane from my head," I typed.

"You just need to let time pass," typed Shannon. "Distance yourself from this."

"Maybe I shouldn't think of this in terms of right or wrong," I typed. "It's more, like, I took a decision, and that decision has different pros and cons, different consequences, than not taking it."

"That was actually great, right?" typed Shannon. "The talk you guys had? You got to express what you were thinking. It seems like both of you handled it well. I would have lost my shit."

"Yeah," I typed. "We were both pretty calm. It's like we were talking about golf or something."

"To be honest, I am still not sure why you didn't go for it, but that's your thing," typed Shannon.

"It's complicated," I typed. "I still feel awkward when people have a crush on me. I don't have a crush on me."

"Well, get over it," typed Shannon. "That's exactly why it would be good for you."

"But the main thing is that at this point, I didn't feel confident this would end in anything other than failure," I typed. "I didn't want us to fuck up and feel awkward and then stop talking. So many people have come in and out of my life this year. It's like I am hemorrhaging people. I don't even know who will be around six months from now."

"I'll still be around six months from now," typed Shannon.

"I hope so," I typed. "I am less worried about us. We're not romantically interested in each other. That makes us invincible. I mean, there's never been any tension between us or anything."

"I had a sex dream about you one time, did I ever tell you that?" typed Shannon.

"Really?" I typed.

"Well, no," typed Shannon. "I mean, to call it a sex dream might be pushing it. All I remember from it is that we were hanging out alone in a room while a party was going on in other rooms, and you were bragging that you had a big one, and then I asked you to show me."

"What happened then?" I typed.

"You pulled down your pants," typed Shannon. "You did. You had a big one."

"That's nice of your imagination," I typed.

"She gives everyone a big one," typed Shannon.

"You know when you dream of specific people," I typed, "but then in the dream they don't behave the same way they do in real life, because they're not themselves, they're controlled by your subconscious? Then you wake up and you're like, 'That bitch, she was so mean to me for no reason.' And if you happen to run into that person, it's like you're still mad a little."

"That used to happen to me with Brian all the time," typed Shannon. "Except the opposite. He was sweet to me in my dreams."

"Did Brian ever write back to you?" I typed. "You haven't mentioned him in a while. I am guessing he hasn't. You would have brought it up."

"No," typed Shannon. "I am chasing an invisible man. I waited and waited and felt all this anxiety and he just decided to stop writing back without even telling me."

"Where's Romy's anxiety pamphlet when we need it?" I typed.

"What?" typed Shannon.

"She has a pamphlet about anxiety in her purse," I typed.

"That would come in handy," typed Shannon. "Do you want to

watch *Shawshank Redemption*? I started watching movies from a list of the top 250 films of all time. The next one is *Shawshank Redemption*."

"Which one is *Shawshank Redemption* again?" I typed. "Is it kind of like *Pocahontas*?"

"It's a prison movie," typed Shannon. "So probably not like *Pocahontas*. Ideally, I would go out, but I can't for the life of me get out of bed right now. I am the worst."

"It's okay," I typed. "We're both the worst."

Unscrew my penis and replace it with a take a penny, leave a penny tray.

The reading I was performing at was taking place in an art gallery. It was the last Wednesday of November and the space had a kind of oppressive presence, one that made me feel as if I should be quiet, exist minimally. "Terrible family road trips in the van," I thought. I talked to Shannon while waiting for things to get started, but was so afraid of running out of saliva that I drank water from a water bottle almost non-stop.

"Thank you so much for coming," I said.

"I am excited to see you read," said Shannon. "There's a lot of people here. I didn't think reading series were this popular."

"My teacher, the one who's curating this," I said. "I think people are afraid of him a little. That's why they're here."

"Well, in any case," said Shannon. "It's a good space. Good crowd."

About ten minutes later, the reading began. I was going third. I sat through the first two performers and didn't pay attention, obsessively went over what I was going to read instead. Then a person announced that I was now going to perform and read a long and overly formal and completely unnecessary introduction and I stood up from my seat and walked to the stage. Holding the microphone, I stared at the audience and felt intimidated a little. I wanted to tuck myself into a ball, hide underneath a chair. I thought, "Don't look at the crowd directly, just look down at your poem and concentrate on it and never look up." I began reading. I heard the crowd laugh at certain lines, which was the desired effect. "I think I want to look," I thought midway through my first piece. "No, just keep going." I knew where Shannon was sitting, so I decided to peek at Shannon briefly, to see how she was responding. I glanced at Shannon, who was grinning, nodding. "This is going okay," I thought. I finished my first poem and read a second poem and then a third poem. Later, I said, "Thank you," in the microphone to indicate that I was done. I walked back to my seat while the crowd applauded. I sat down and couldn't think any particular thought, as if my skull had been hollowed out, like a pumpkin.

After the reading ended, some people came up to me. One person shook my hand and said, "You were very good," and it felt like I had just made love to this person, even though I hadn't met this person before.

If you're not feeling anxiety, you're part of someone else's anxiety.

It snowed as if a spare planet had been pulverized into tiny bits and a fine powder.

The past was there to be accessed.

The first week of December, I stopped by the house to return my house key, something I had been meaning to do, but kept putting off. I looked around and saw that Ines' room was empty and that Cristian's room was also empty. In the bathroom, I noticed the machine gun above the shower head was gone. "Oh, hey," said Brent, coming out of his room. We sat in the common area, chatted a little. "Cristian moved back in with his mom," said Brent. "He wasn't happy about it." I asked Brent if he had found a place to live and he said that he was still looking, but that most of his stuff was already packed and that he was ready to go. Later, I left my key on the kitchen table and then absentmindedly looked out the window. The body image statue stared back at me.

The more I thought about it, the more I felt like video games and poems had a lot in common. They both tended to take themselves seriously, without caring whether or not the player or reader would be accepting them on those terms. In the story mode of any given Call of Duty, part of the pleasure, for me, came from making fun of the game as I played it, for taking itself so seriously. I sometimes experienced a similar kind of disconnect when reading poems, between the emotional landscape of the poem and my emotional landscape while reading it.

Video games were also often about the player achieving salvation, while poems were often about the speaker achieving salvation.

Staring at my computer screen, I suddenly wanted to fold my Facebook into an origami crane.

"Lots of goddamn cats here," read a text message from Cristian.

I looked at the bottom right corner of my screen as if hoping to be told that my work shift was now over, but then I was already home and this was just life.

I received a text message from Cristian asking what I was doing. It was late December. I replied with the address of the party I was at, in the back of a building located on a side street. After confirming that he was on his way, Cristian sent me a picture taken with his phone, along with a caption that read "Ice rink, phase one." The picture seemed to be of partly frozen water, a tree and a wooden fence at night.

About two hours later, we hugged and then sat on the ground in a hallway outside the space.

"Do you have a cigarette?" said Cristian.

"I never buy packs," I said.

"Oh, that's right," said Cristian. "I forgot. I'll just find one later."

"You built the ice rink," I said.

"You should see it," said Cristian. "It started as an excuse to avoid being around my mom. Her backyard is a lot smaller than the one at the house, and I don't even know if people will actually come skating on it, but I am almost done."

"I didn't think you would actually build it, to be honest," I said. "I thought you would just talk about doing it until it was too late."

"I had no idea what I was getting myself into," said Cristian. "It's not just spraying water and waiting for it to freeze. It's more complicated than that."

"How long did it take you?" I said.

"It's so much work, it's insane," said Cristian. "The ice rink is my full-time job right now. That's on top of my part-time job, which is my part-time job."

"You should have a little opening party," I said. "Show it off."

"Yeah," said Cristian. He laughed. "I should have a ribbon-cutting ceremony."

"That would be funny," I said. "I would come to that."

I continued chatting with Cristian for about an hour. Then I saw Romy from afar. Her hair was a different colour and she was wearing a gray sweater and dark-coloured tights. We waved at one another calmly. I stood up.

"Thomas," said Romy.

"Rosemary," I said in a mock formal tone.

"Don't call me that," said Romy. She smiled. "I thought about you today. We lost our power for a while. I thought our electricity had been cut off, but it was just a power outage. There's a number you can call. A robot asks for your information and then it tells you if the power being out is normal or not. The robot was trying really hard to pretend it was a person. It was cute."

"It sounds cute," I said. "I like the hair."

"Thank you," said Romy. "Are you going in?"

"Maybe later," I said.

"Okay," said Romy. "I'll see you later."

I nodded. I wanted to talk to Cristian some more, but then turned around and couldn't find him. "Maybe he went outside to look for a cigarette," I thought. I located my backpack and winter jacket and put them on. Outside, there were a few people socializing near the back door, but Cristian wasn't one of them. I stood amongst them and stared at nothing. The cold air felt temporarily refreshing. For no valid reason, I thought about leaving without telling anyone. I stalled, trying to decide whether I should stay or leave.

I thought about how I felt not old, but not young anymore either.

I thought about how I felt like an alien in both English and French.

I thought about how I felt like what I wanted, deep down, was to not get what I wanted.

Those seemed to be my thoughts and feelings.

ESPLANADE
Books

THE FICTION SERIES AT VÉHICULE PRESS

A House by the Sea : A novel by Sikeena Karmali

A Short Journey by Car : Stories by Liam Durcan

Seventeen Tomatoes : Tales from Kashmir : Stories by Jaspreet Singh

Garbage Head : A novel by Christopher Willard

The Rent Collector : A novel by B. Glen Rotchin

Dead Man's Float : A novel by Nicholas Maes

Optique : Stories by Clayton Bailey

Out of Cleveland : Stories by Lolette Kuby

Pardon Our Monsters : Stories by Andrew Hood

Chef : A novel by Jaspreet Singh

Orfeo : A novel by Hans-Jürgen Greif
[Translated by Fred A. Reed]

Anna's Shadow : A novel by David Manicom

Sundre : A novel by Christopher Willard

Animals : A novel by Don LePan

Writing Personals : A novel by Lolette Kuby

Niko : A novel by Dimitri Nasrallah

Stopping for Strangers : Stories by Daniel Griffin

The Love Monster: A novel by Missy Marston

A Message for the Emperor : A novel by Mark Frutkin

New Tab : A novel by Guillaume Morissette

Véhicule Press